Beckett stepped into her personal space.

Her heart bounced off her rib cage and her stomach felt like it was taking a roller-coaster ride, but she'd be damned if she'd let Beck see how much his hot, hard body affected her.

Beck smiled, lifted a hand and rested the tip of his index finger in the V of her throat. "Your pulse is trying to burst through your skin."

Dammit. Damned pulse. *Heart, stop beating.*

Beck's hot fingertip ran up the side of her throat until he reached her jaw. "God, your eyes. My memory didn't do them justice. Silver and green all contained in a ring of emerald."

Cady swallowed and shook her head. "Don't do this, Beckett."

"I think I have to," Beckett replied, the heat of his hand scalding her jaw. His other hand grasped her hip and he pulled her into him.

Beck's lips were pure magic as his mouth took possession of hers. Cady felt his hand cup her right butt cheek and he launched her up into his muscular body. She closed her eyes, not quite believing that he was holding her, that his mouth was on hers. It felt like it belonged there, as if she'd been created to be kissed by him. Beck kissed like he owned her, like she was—just for this moment in time—still his.

* * *

Reunited...and Pregnant is part of The Ballantyne Billionaires series:
A family who has it all...except love!

Dear Reader,

In *His Ex's Well-Kept Secret*—Jaeger's story—I introduced you to the Ballantynes, four siblings who are heirs to a Manhattan-based empire built on luxury gemstones. Raised by their uncle Connor, Jaeger, Beck, Linc and Sage have it all: wealth, prestige, smarts and good looks—and, frequently, complicated notions about love.

Reunited...and Pregnant is Beckett's story. Beckett is one smart cookie, incredibly driven and a relentless workaholic. He's the finance director and troubleshooter for Ballantyne International. A decade ago, his family forced him to take a gap year to travel and he spent two months in Asia with Cady. Beckett, who is such a lone wolf, has issues with falling in love, so when things got too deep with Cady, he sent her back to the United States. But love finds a way and Cady is back in his life, desperate to rescue her business, and running the new Ballantyne PR campaign is how she intends to do that.

Cady has a business to save and a baby to raise—she doesn't have time to revisit the past with the ever-sexy Beck Ballantyne. Or so she thinks...

I'm having such fun writing about the Ballantynes—they keep surprising me—and I very much hope you enjoy them, too!

Happy reading,

Joss

xxx

Connect with me at josswoodbooks.com, Twitter (@josswoodbooks) or Facebook (Joss Wood Author).

JOSS WOOD

REUNITED...AND PREGNANT

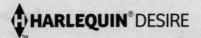

Recycling programs
for this product may
not exist in your area.

ISBN-13: 978-0-373-83850-9

Reunited...and Pregnant

Copyright © 2017 by Joss Wood

All rights reserved. Except for use in any review, the reproduction or utilization of this work in whole or in part in any form by any electronic, mechanical or other means, now known or hereinafter invented, including xerography, photocopying and recording, or in any information storage or retrieval system, is forbidden without the written permission of the publisher, Harlequin Enterprises Limited, 225 Duncan Mill Road, Don Mills, Ontario M3B 3K9, Canada.

This is a work of fiction. Names, characters, places and incidents are either the product of the author's imagination or are used fictitiously, and any resemblance to actual persons, living or dead, business establishments, events or locales is entirely coincidental.

This edition published by arrangement with Harlequin Books S.A.

For questions and comments about the quality of this book, please contact us at CustomerService@Harlequin.com.

® and TM are trademarks of Harlequin Enterprises Limited or its corporate affiliates. Trademarks indicated with ® are registered in the United States Patent and Trademark Office, the Canadian Intellectual Property Office and in other countries.

Printed in U.S.A.

Joss Wood loves books and traveling—especially to the wild places of southern Africa. She has the domestic skills of a potted plant and drinks far too much coffee.

Joss has written for Harlequin KISS, Harlequin Presents and, most recently, the Harlequin Desire line. After a career in business, she now writes full-time. Joss is a member of the Romance Writers of America and Romance Writers of South Africa.

Books by Joss Wood

Harlequin Desire

Taking the Boss to Bed

From Mavericks to Married

Trapped with the Maverick Millionaire
Pregnant by the Maverick Millionaire
Married to the Maverick Millionaire

The Ballantyne Billionaires

His Ex's Well-Kept Secret
Reunited...and Pregnant

Visit her Author Profile page at Harlequin.com, or josswoodbooks.com, for more titles.

To the reader: thank you for spending your precious time with my characters.

Prologue

In Bangkok International Airport, Beckett Ballantyne, his booted feet resting on his backpack, looked across the row of seats to Cady and smiled. Her eyes were closed, her lips moving as she silently sang along to whatever she was listening to via the new pair of earbuds she'd bought in Pantip Plaza yesterday.

A light green bandeau held her long, deep brown hair off her face and turned her wintry eyes a light green. Sitting with her heels on the seat of her chair and wearing denim shorts, a white tank and beaded bracelets, she looked exactly like what she was: a sexy backpacker seeing the world.

With that half smile on her face, the flirt of a dimple in her cheek, she would make anyone looking at her envious of her freedom, jealous of her next adventure.

She was young, gorgeous and adventurous and, no one, Beck was certain, would suspect that she was utterly miserable.

Not with him. They were, as far as he knew, perfectly fine for a couple who'd met and run off to South East Asia together within a month of meeting at an off-campus party in New York. Technically, since his trip was planned, she'd run off, choosing to spend the long summer holidays after freshman year traveling with him.

Her staid, conservative, churchy parents had freaked.

Beck glanced at the phone in her hand and he wondered how many emails and voice messages they'd left, begging her to come home. How many tears would she shed this time? How long would it take her to come out of the funk their recriminations tossed her into?

In Beckett's mind it was psychological torture, and her parents just kept up the pressure. She was wasting her life; she was a disrespectful daughter; she was living in sin with him...

Her father had an ulcer; her mother was depressed. How could she be enjoying her trip when they were so miserable? They missed her and worried constantly about her—what if she was kidnapped and sold into the sex trade? They'd heard there was a bomb blast in Thailand—what if she was caught up in an explosion?

He'd told her to ignore them, to only check in once a week, but Cady couldn't disconnect. Their mind games turned her into a conflicted mess. She wanted to be with him but her guilt over disappointing her parents was eating her from the inside out.

He knew that she felt stuck in the middle. He thought her parents were narrow-minded and they thought he was a spoiled rich kid, the spawn of Satan because he lured their innocent daughter overseas with the sole intention of corrupting her.

If one could call worshipping her body at every opportunity corruption…

Beck felt the action in his pants and tipped his head back to look at the ceiling, readily admitting that he couldn't get enough of Cady. At twenty-three, he'd had other lovers, so he couldn't understand why he was utterly addicted to making love with her, being with her.

If he believed in the emotion, he might think that he was in love. But since he didn't, wouldn't allow himself to, he did what he always did and pushed those uncomfortable thoughts away.

Her parents' disapproval would've been easier for Cady to handle if she genuinely loved traveling, loved experiencing the hugely different cultures they stepped into. But having been protected and co-cooned, she'd cried at the poverty and slums she saw in India, been shocked by the sex trade in Phuket. The crowds, the sounds and strange food threw her, and the lack of English disoriented her. He couldn't fault her for trying, and she didn't whine but she wasn't enjoying the experience. It didn't help that she'd had her wallet lifted, her butt touched and had to spend four days in a grungy bathroom, her arms wrapped around a cracked toilet bowl.

He'd thought she'd enjoy the clear sea and white-sand beaches of Phi Phi, the island they'd just returned from. But Cady was miserable. And because Cady was miserable, he was, too. He'd thought that their desperate need to be with each other could conquer anything.

He was so wrong.

With his ridiculously high IQ, being wrong was not a concept he was very familiar with.

God, these last two weeks together would be torture. Every time he thought of her leaving, his stomach knotted and his lungs seized. They had a plan, he reminded himself; they'd agreed to three months together and then she'd head back to college and he'd continue his travels.

But after two and a half months together, he knew that he could no longer take her, and his feelings for her, lightly. And that realization made him feel like his life was spinning out of control. While his little brain was already mourning her departure, his big brain was insisting they could do with some distance, some time apart. He needed a lot of space and quite a bit of time apart because he was starting to suspect that she might be the beat of his heart, the breath on his lips, the reason the sun rose in the morning.

He had to let her go because, if he wasn't careful, he could love her with a fierce, crazy, forever type of love. Love like that meant taking a very real risk, a huge leap of faith. It made him feel lost, exposed and far too vulnerable—all the emotions he'd been trying to avoid since he was eight. Love meant pain, and he was too smart to put himself in harm's way.

Love meant losing control.

Love was also, it was said, supposed to make you feel happy and complete. He didn't deserve to feel happy and he'd never feel complete. How could he when he was the reason his parents' remains, and those of his unborn sibling, were scattered on a mountain in Vermont?

Beck felt his cell phone vibrate in his back pocket and pulled it out. He smiled at the name on the display. He had two older brothers, Linc through adoption and Jaeger through birth, and he loved them equally.

They were also equally annoying in their belief that he needed looking after. The fact that he was taller and bigger than both of them didn't stop them fussing over him and his younger sister, Sage.

This time it was Jaeger calling.

"Jay, what's up?" he asked after answering the call.

"Just checking up on you. Any trouble?"

Beck rolled his eyes. He wasn't that stupid; he wasn't stupid at all. "Actually, I was just about to call you. We're sitting in a Thai jail. They found some coke on us."

There was long silence before Jaeger released a harsh curse. "That's not funny, Beck."

Beck grinned. "I thought it was."

"You are *such* an ass."

Beck tapped Cady on her knee and pointed to his backpack, silently telling her to keep an eye on his stuff. She nodded and Beck stood up to walk toward the window looking out onto the busy tarmac.

"Where are you? Bangkok?" Jaeger asked. "And are you still heading for Vietnam?"

"That's the plan, why?"

"I'm heading there day after next. I've had a tip about a new rustic mine in Yen Bai producing some very high quality rubies. Want to come with me and see what we can buy?"

Beck felt a spurt of excitement, the kick of adrenaline at the thought of hunting gems with his brother to supply the demands of Ballantyne's rich and demanding clients. "Hell, yes."

Then he remembered that he wasn't traveling alone. "Can I bring Cady?"

"I'm not sure of the area, Beck. I wouldn't," Jaeger replied. "Can't she stay in Hanoi by herself for a couple of days?"

Beck ran his hand over the back of his neck. The backpackers they'd met on Phi Phi were heading to Hanoi, as well, and they were all staying at the same backpacker's hostel. Maybe they—and their new friend Amy especially—could keep an eye on Cady for a few days. He was fairly certain she'd be okay.

Then the disapproving faces of Cady's parents jumped onto the big screen of his mind and he instantly felt guilty. He was responsible for Cady, not Amy.

"Let me think about it," he told Jaeger. But he knew he couldn't leave Cady in Hanoi by herself.

"No worries," Jaeger replied. "I'm glad that you've reconciled yourself to traveling. Connor was worried that you wouldn't but I knew that our parents' adventurous spirit was still in you, albeit deeply buried."

"It's not like I have a choice, Jaeger. That was the ultimatum Connor and Linc gave me, supported by you, I might add."

Yeah, he enjoyed traveling but he was still pissed that his uncle and his brothers refused to allow him to join Ballantyne's until he'd taken a gap year or two.

"You know why, Beck," Jaeger said, his deep voice low and concerned. "You've been operating at warp speed since you were a kid. You finished school early, partly because you're brilliant, but mostly because you worked your tail off. You made the national swim championships because every moment you weren't studying you were in the pool. When you gave up competitive swimming we thanked God because we thought you might finally get a life. Date some girls, have some fun, get into some trouble. Not you. You went off to college and got your master's in business in record time. You're twenty-three years old and you've spent the past ten years working your ass off. If you come back to Ballantyne's, you'll do exactly the same thing. So we don't care if you sit on a beach for the next eight months or if you enter an ashram, but what you aren't doing is going straight to work."

Beck gripped the bridge of his nose with his thumb and forefinger. He'd heard this lecture a hundred times before.

"Anyway, this is a stupid conversation because we all know that you love traveling."

He did. He loved the freedom it gave him, loved the anonymity. While traveling, he was Beck, no surname attached. For the first time in fifteen years he felt marginally free, a little at peace, a lot chilled.

"Do you think that tying yourself to Cady while you travel is a good idea?" Jaeger asked.

"What are you talking about?"

Beck glanced at Cady, who met his eyes and gave him that quick, sunburst smile that always jump-started his heart.

"According to her social media posts, she's ditching school and spending the next year traveling with you."

What the hell...?

"She's going back to school," Beck said, forcing the words up his tight throat.

"Uh...not according to Sage, who follows both of you on social media. It was girl speak...something about her loving you enough to continue traveling with you."

A large bead of sweat rolled down his temple and into his heavy stubble. A loud bell clanged in his ears, and his stomach felt like it had taken a ride on a death-defying roller coaster.

That wasn't the plan. He needed them to stick to the plan.

"That's not happening." He managed, through his panic, to push the words out.

"Look," Jaeger said, impatient, "I've got more important things to do than talk about your love life. Just let me know about ruby-hunting in Yen Bai."

Using his phone, Beck pulled up her social media account and yep, Cady had posted something about not returning to college and extending her trip with him.

Beck pocketed his phone and gripped the railing separating him from the floor-to-ceiling windows. He dropped his head and stared at his grubby boots. Fear, hot and acidic, burned a ring of fire around his heart, up his throat and coated his mouth in a bitter film.

She was supposed to be a three-month fling. This wasn't supposed to get this intense, this quickly. He'd been banking on her going home, heading back to college. Her leaving had been his safety net, the way he stopped himself from falling all the way in love with her. If she stayed with him, he doubted he could resist her and then he'd be up crap creek in a sinking canoe.

He wasn't prepared to go there. If he loved her and lost her…

Hell, no. Not happening.

Why hadn't she spoken to him first before blabbing online? He knew that her choosing him over her parents was her way of making a statement but hell, hers wasn't the only seat on this train. He had a right to decide whether he wanted to keep traveling with her. He couldn't bear to see her go but he couldn't risk his heart by her staying.

Devil, meet the deep blue sea.

The only rational option, his instinctive reaction, was to stick to the plan they'd decided on back in New York. She needed to go home, go back to college and he'd see her at Christmas. The only deviation he was prepared to make to that plan was to send her home as quickly as possible. They were in an airport and that could be accomplished right now.

Because if he didn't walk away today, he knew that he never would.

His decision made, Beck walked over to her and picked up his backpack with one hand and grabbed hers with another.

Cady pulled out the earbuds and slung her smaller backpack over her shoulder as she stood up. "What's up?"

When Beck gestured to the familiar logo of an American carrier at the neighboring gate, her eyes flashed with joy. "Oh, my God, we're going home?" she squealed, dancing on the spot.

He just looked at her, wanting her to understand without having to say the words. After a little confused silence, the light faded from her eyes and color leached from her face. "You're not coming with me?"

Beck shook his head.

He dropped the backpacks at his feet and slapped his hands on his hips. It took him a while to find the words he needed. "Jaeger wants me to meet him in

Vietnam to look for rubies with him, and you can't come with, and I can't leave you on your own."

Cady's bottom lip trembled and she rocked on her heels, looking like he'd sideswiped her with a stick, but he continued. "It's only two weeks early, Cady, and it's not like you were enjoying yourself."

"I love spending time with you! In fact, I had just decided that I want to stay, to ignore my folks' disapproval, to get into the hang of this. I want to be with—"

Beck jumped in before she could finish that sentence. "You're going back to school, Cady. That was always the plan. I'm just sending you home two weeks early."

Cady took a step back and her eyes filled with tears. "You're *sending* me home?"

Oh, damn, bad choice of words. "I'll be home for Christmas. We can reevaluate then."

"You're sending me home?" Cady repeated his words, emphasizing each one.

"Christmas is in three months—"

Cady's lips firmed and she folded her arms across her torso. "Do you love me, Beck?" she demanded.

Ah, no. Not this question. He could love her, he silently admitted, and that was why she needed to go back to the States. Falling in love with Cady, with anyone, wasn't something he was prepared to do.

When he didn't answer, Cady grabbed his arm, her nails digging into his skin.

Beck jerked his arm away and forced himself to meet her eyes. Oh, damn, he wished he hadn't because, as long as he lived, he'd remember the betrayal he saw within them, the pain he'd caused. Cady lifted her hand to grab the fabric of his shirt just above his heart, twisting it in her fist. "Don't do this, Beck. Don't throw us away, don't toss me aside. We can fix this."

"That's the thing, Cades, I can't be fixed."

It was a special type of hell, Beck thought, to watch a heart break. It was even worse when you were responsible for it breaking.

One

Almost a decade later

Sitting at one of the many high tables in Bonnets, a swish cocktail bar just off Fifth Avenue, Cady Collins had to physically stop herself from appropriating the massive salt-rimmed margarita delivered to the table next to her. The taste buds on the back of her tongue tingled as she imagined the perfect combination of salt and the sugar-tinged tang of tequila.

It had been a tequila type of day and week. Year.

The waiter turned to her, lifted an eyebrow at her empty glass. "Another virgin Bloody Mary?"

God, Friday night and she was in the most reviewed cocktail bar in the city—the joke was that

Bonnets had the license to serve cocktails to the angels—and she was drinking tomato juice.

How sad.

Cady saw the screen of her phone light up, saw the display say The Boss and sighed as she lifted the device to her ear. "Hi, Mom."

"Cady, where are you?" Edna Collins asked in her best I'm-the-preacher's-wife voice.

Cady resisted the urge to tell her that she was in a bar tucking dollar bills into the tiny thong of a muscled, oiled male stripper. *You're an adult. You don't need to try to shock your parents anymore.*

"What's the matter, Mom?"

Edna called her at precisely 8:00 p.m. every second Sunday. A call outside that time meant that something had rattled The Force.

"You might have heard that the preacher at our sister church in Wilton is retiring and the church has been looking for a suitable replacement."

Not really. She didn't keep up with what was happening in the exciting world of church politics in upstate New York.

Cady sent another look at the icy margarita and felt her mouth tingle. One little sip... How much damage could one sip do?

"Your father is being considered."

"Good for him," Cady replied because she was expected to say something.

"We need you to come home in two weeks," Edna stated, her voice suggesting that an argument would not be tolerated.

"Me? Why?"

"Your father is undergoing a process of rigorous interviews. I will be interviewed, as well. As you are our only child, they want to meet you, too."

Cady wanted to tell her mother that she wasn't an only child, that she'd had a brother, that his life mattered, but as always she refrained. Will wasn't someone they regularly discussed. Or at all.

"Mother, what possible bearing could I have on the proceedings? I live in New York City, and I rarely come home."

"You never come home," Edna corrected.

That might be because home was the place where she had no wiggle room, where there was no room for error. Home was a place of pressure, with a lot of interest shown but little love. After Will was sent away, she'd lived in constant fear that she would be, too.

Home was hymnal music and stockings, religious books and piety.

Cady shuddered. "Well, sorry. That's not going to happen."

Cady heard her mother's shocked gasp. "But you have to! Not meeting with the interview committee would reflect very badly on your father and his chance to secure this position. It's a big church, Cady, with a lot of resources. Since you put that traveling nonsense behind you, you've been a model daughter, a credit to us. Highly educated, with your own business. I have no doubt you are an example to others in that sin-filled city."

Yeah, Cady Collins, the beacon for clean living. Oh, God, her mother was going to die when she heard her latest news. As for that traveling nonsense, her time in Thailand with Beck was the only time she felt completely herself. Free.

Loved. For a brief moment in time, she'd felt so loved.

"It would be a huge step up for him," her mother droned on. "And when they meet you, they'll have the proof that we have raised a God-fearing, smart young woman who has her feet firmly on the ground."

If the statement wasn't so sad, she'd roll on the floor and wet herself laughing. "Mom, trust me, you really don't want me there. Find an excuse and we'll save a lot of trouble."

"I have no idea what you're rambling about and I don't have the time to argue with you. We have guests for dinner. Do not disappoint us, Cady," Edna snapped before she disconnected.

Cady gently tapped the corner of her phone against the tabletop. She'd left home more than a decade ago, but the urge to please her parents was still strong. In their small rural town in upstate New York, she'd been the popular pastor's kid. Honor student, cheerleader, student council president, homecoming queen. Pretty, popular, nice. As perfect as she could possibly be.

She said "please" and "thank you" and "excuse me" and ran errands and never missed church. She didn't smoke or drink or party or date because she was an "example." She'd never had the chance to be a regular kid, to mess up, to fail.

The pressure to be perfect was immense and it was generally accepted that she became an over-achiever because that was what her parents expected. Sure, that was part of the reason, but no one knew that she was terrified of messing up, of doing or saying the wrong thing.

Of being banished like Will, her older brother.

As a result, her desire to please her parents still lingered. They wouldn't be very impressed with her now, she thought, reflecting on the trouble she'd landed herself in. Then again, she was fairly sure that Edna and Bill Collins had been expecting her to mess up again since she'd run off to Southeast Asia with Beck Ballantyne nine years before. She'd wanted to be with Beck more than she'd wanted to please her mom and dad and...*boom*! Fireworks.

This latest bombshell would rock their world again. Cady pushed the tips of her fingers into her forehead and held back a whimper. And that was without telling them that her business was rocky and she was running out of options to keep it on the rails.

"Cady?"

Cady jerked her head up to see a small blonde and a tall brunette standing next to her table. The blonde looked familiar, but she instantly recognized the classic good looks of Julia Parker, a Fortune 500 business consultant who socialized with the great and good of New York society. Cady would never forget Julia, especially since the woman had recently convinced Trott's Sports—a corporate sports store that was one of two clients that paid Cady a hefty monthly retainer—to not renew their contract with Collins Consulting.

Thank God she was still contracted to Natural Fuel, Tom's company, a chain of health food outlets, to handle their media releases and promotions. Without that contract, she'd be sunk.

Losing Trott's had left her with a sizable hole in her business bank account. And without her biggest client. Cady resisted the urge to toss her tomato juice over Julia's pristine white dress and instead held out her hand to shake. God, sometimes being an adult sucked.

"Cady Collins, Collins Consulting."

Julia immediately made the connection.

"Trott's... They couldn't afford to renew," Julia murmured, and wrinkled her nose. "Sorry."

Cady shrugged.

"Are you doing okay?"

Julia's question surprised her; she didn't expect her to ask or to sound like she cared. Cady lifted her hands up in a "what can I do" gesture. "It's tough."

"For what it's worth, I like your work," Julia stated, and Cady heard and appreciated the sincerity in her statement.

"Thank you."

"You don't recognize me, do you?" the blonde demanded, pulling their attention back to her, her smile bright and big.

Cady shook her head.

"I'm Amy Cook. We met on Phi Phi island when you were traveling with Beck years ago."

Beck. Funny, she'd just been thinking about him. *Like that's a coincidence,* Cady mocked herself. *You've been thinking about the man, pretty much constantly, for the best part of the last decade.*

Cady cocked her head and peered at the woman. The image of her with waist-length blond hair and a thong bikini popped into her head. "I remember you. You flirted shamelessly with Beck."

"She flirts with everyone. Don't take it personally," Julia said, a rich chuckle following her words.

"Do you live in Manhattan?" Amy demanded. "What do you do? Are you married? Do you have children?"

Cady didn't know which question to answer first. Work was easy, the other questions were a tad more complicated. "Um… I live in Brooklyn and I have my own PR company."

Amy's eyes widened. "Really? Seriously?"

Millions of women worked in PR and many owned their own companies. Why was this such a surprise? Speaking of business, she desperately needed to drum up some, and it wasn't every day that she bumped into one of the best business consultants in the city, so Cady reached into her tote bag and pulled out a business card.

She handed Julia the card with a small shrug. "I'd be grateful if you kept me in mind if any of your clients need PR or any marketing help. I'm good, efficient and reasonable."

Julia took the card from her and nodded. "I'll do that."

Amy cocked her head, and her dark brown eyes connected with Cady's. "You didn't tell me if you're married or if you have children."

Yeah, right. She was not discussing any of those thorny subjects with a woman she'd exchanged ten words with nearly ten years ago.

Cady looked at the entrance of Bonnets and faked a smile. "Ah, the person I'm waiting for has arrived. It was interesting running into you again, Amy. Nice to meet you, Julia."

"But—" Amy protested.

"Come on." Julia placed a hand on Amy's back and pushed her away. "Let's find someone else you can practice your CIA interrogation skills on."

Cady rolled her eyes. Of all the people in the world she'd thought she'd never see again, and whom she never wanted to see again, Amy was at the top of her list. Nearly a decade ago, Beck had tired of Cady and he'd sent her home so that he could sow his wild oats all over the Asian subcontinent. Once Cady left, she was sure Amy had stepped right on into the space, in bed and out, that Cady had occupied in Beck's life.

Beck had been and still was the honey that female bees flocked to. She watched his subtle flirting, heard him laughing with Amy, and she'd felt like she couldn't compete with the blonde bombshell.

Cady was long, lanky and not overly blessed, as her boyfriend, Tom, told her often enough, in the "boobage" department. But it was more than that. Beck, Amy and the other backpackers they'd met had been just so together, so effortlessly confident. Of course, there were the stoners and weirdos and the lost, but many of the travelers had their lives sorted. They were street-smart and confident and knew where they were going and what to do when they got there.

Thanks to her protected, insulated childhood, she would've been utterly lost without Beck making the decisions for her. Was that why he'd ditched her, because she'd been lacking in self-confidence and because she'd become more of a responsibility than a girlfriend?

Who knew? He'd been long on termination and short on explanations. He'd just handed her a ticket and stood in line with her at Passport Control. When she'd cleared that, she'd turned back to look at him through the glass walls and saw him walking away, taking a fair share of her shattered heart with him.

"Cady."

Cady looked up and accepted Tom's quick brush of his lips against her cheek. He sat down opposite her and immediately glanced at his watch. "I have about a half hour before I need to be back in the office. Can we make this quick?"

Wow, nice to see you, too, Tom. "I thought we were having dinner together?"

"Can't. I have some problems at work, so I need to get back to my desk."

She was sleeping with her client, and the fact that she was still embarrassed her. Tom dismissed her concerns of their lack of professionalism, saying they were both single and it wasn't a hanging offense. She'd tried to be okay with it but she'd finally made the decision to call it quits. Fate, however, had other ideas.

"You look like hell, Cady. What's up with that?"

Tom's jerk quotient always went up when he was stressed, Cady thought. It wasn't personal, she reminded herself.

But it sure felt pretty personal. Beck had hurt her when he tossed her away, but he'd never talked to her like this. Then again, Tom Steel wasn't Beck Ballantyne. Nobody could be.

Gorgeous, super-smart and highly successful, he'd set the bar pretty high and no man could reach it.

Let's get some perspective here, Collins. Beck kicked you out of his life; he sent you away. You expected it from your parents, but not from the man you loved to distraction. Who you thought might love you.

That had been a very erroneous assumption.

Tom's flat hand hitting the table jolted her back into the present. "Cady! Just say what you have to say, will you?"

Sure.

"I'm pregnant."

Tom's low, vicious curse hung in the air between them. "Get rid of it."

She'd somehow expected him to say that. "Not an option."

Her parents had rid themselves of Will by sending

him to live at a residential home when he was thirteen, and Beck had sent her away, too, but she was not prepared to do the same to her child. Sure, a pregnancy wasn't convenient, but neither had Will's autism or her falling in love with Beck been convenient.

You didn't just erase the problem because you didn't like the outcome.

Tom's face turned paper-white. "I need a drink."

Cady watched Tom walk to the bar and hoped that her baby didn't inherit his knock-kneed walk. Or his lack of height. Or the cowlick just above his right ear.

He isn't Beck...

Damn him for being the entire package, both smart and sexy. A blue-eyed wavy haired blond, Beck looked like he belonged on the cover of a surfing magazine. Long-limbed and muscular, he looked as good in a tuxedo as he did in a pair of swimming shorts. Unlike Beckett, Tom didn't make her head swim or her heart race and she liked it that way. It was an adult relationship with no teenage hormones and irrationality to cloud her thinking. She certainly never felt short of breath or felt the need to rip Tom's clothes off.

She'd been careful with Tom; she hadn't given him any of her heart. She'd given Beckett everything—including her virginity—only to be dismissed when he'd had enough of her.

So, yeah, Tom never set her panties, or her heart, on fire and walking away from him was going to be easy. She'd just prefer not to be pregnant while she did it.

Single and pregnant. Her parents were going to be so proud.

Cady rested her hand on her stomach. There was only one fact of which she was certain: she was keeping her baby.

Tom banged his tumbler of whiskey onto the table and sat down again. He lifted his glass to his lips and sent her a long, cold look.

"Is it mine?"

Cady lifted her hands in the air. "Are you crazy? Of course it's yours. I haven't slept with anyone else but you since we started dating."

Tom shrugged. He turned his head toward the bar, leered at a new female arrival and turned back to her, looking supremely disinterested.

"The baby is yours, Tom," Cady repeated, enunciating the words.

He pouted. "So you say."

"Tom, we've been seeing each other for the best part of a year."

"I didn't think we were dating *only* each other."

Cady blinked, utterly astounded. What the hell?

Wait, hold on a second... If Tom thought that they weren't exclusive then that meant that he had colored outside the lines, so to speak. "Have you cheated on me?"

"Since I didn't think we were exclusive I don't consider it cheating."

"You bastard!" Cady stopped herself from banging the table. "Who?"

"Does it matter?" Tom asked, his voice cool. He

motioned to her stomach, and his next words cata-
pulted this exchange from a bad dream into a nightmare. "Get rid of it or you're fired."

"You can't fire me. I have a contract with you!"
Cady stated, not recognizing the cold, heartless man
sitting opposite her. God, if she lost Tom's business,
as well…

"So sue me." Tom shrugged, unconcerned. "I'll
win. Cady, I'm not interested in having a baby. If
you want child support you're going to have to sue
me for that, as well," Tom stated after draining his
glass of whiskey. "But I should warn you that I'll sic
both sets of lawyers on you—mine and my wife's."

What? His *wife's* lawyers? He was divorced; he'd
been divorced for a little over a year. He'd divorced her
because she'd refused to date him until he was free.

Oh, dear God…

"You called Gretchen your wife." Cady forced
the question through her now-numb lips. "Have you
been cheating on me with your wife?"

Tom's cold look pushed ice into her bones. "Cady,
I never divorced her. I've been cheating on her…
with you."

After sending a text message to the group name
"family" on his phone—telling them he was fine and
enjoying his trip—Beck sat down at the desk in his
luxury hotel room to Skype Amy.

His computer did its thing and then Amy's pixie
face filled his screen. She scowled at him. "It's about
time you called."

"Hello to you, too," Beck said with a faint smile. Beck wondered, not for the first time, who was the boss in the relationship. He might be a Ballantyne director, but Amy, the PA he shared with Linc and the person he and his siblings entrusted with the most confidential information, was the power behind the throne. "What's up?"

"So much," Amy answered and held up her index finger. "Don't go away. I'm just going to get my wine."

Beck laughed when Julia hung her face, upside down, over the screen to blow him a kiss. Amy's long-term partner and soon-to-be wife was a goofball, and around her loved ones, she rarely acted like the cool professional the financial world knew her to be.

Beck picked up his laptop, walked toward the bed and placed the device on the bedside table. He tucked pillows between his head and the headboard of the massive bed and stretched out his legs. He liked beds to be big enough to accommodate his six-four frame.

Beck placed his laptop on his knees and reached for his beer. He sipped it as he watched Amy's cat, Lazy Joe, jump with great effort onto her chair and curl up into a gray-and-white ball. Amy returned, picked up the cat and resettled the feline on her lap.

"God, look at you with your messy hair and your stubble, wearing only a pair of track pants. So hot." Amy tossed a quick look over her shoulder. "Julia, I'm thinking of going straight."

"Stop lusting over Beckett, you pervert. He's your

boss." Julia's voice drifted over from the kitchen, sounding perfectly relaxed.

"And you're not my type. Even if you were straight we'd have no chemistry," Beck said mildly.

"True. So, I'm now going to ignore that fabulous chest and six-pack abs."

"So kind," Beck murmured.

"You look like you're having a miserable time on your forced break," Amy commented.

After his first year of working for Ballantyne International, Connor had insisted that, because he was a driven, relentless workaholic with a habit of working sixteen or more hours a day, he take a week off every four months. Initially, he'd felt like Connor was punishing him for working too hard, but he eventually realized that it was his uncle's way of looking after his health. Connor knew that he couldn't force Beck to stop working but he could at least manage him.

No one did that now. Connor's death had leveled the playing fields between him and his brothers and he no longer took orders that he not work so hard. His siblings didn't understand, and he'd never explain, that he liked to work insane hours, that his devotion to Ballantyne International was his way of showing them that he was an asset to the company, his way to earn and keep his place in his family.

"It was the kid's fault. He asked them to come home. He'd broken his wrist and he needed to have it pinned and made a big deal about them coming home to be with him."

"Which one is he?"

"Can't see him right now. But he's the middle child, the one who had a panic attack in church."

"Two lives and a baby on the way—a hell of a price to pay for a broken arm. I wonder if he'll ever know the damage his whining caused."

Because Beck was under the table, hidden by the long tablecloth, and listening to the whispered conversations of the mourners invited back to the family home after the funeral, he heard the comments and understood perfectly. His parents' deaths were his fault.

It was a conclusion he'd already come to. Hearing it spoken aloud just confirmed what he already thought. From that day on, he'd always felt like the outsider looking in and he'd made himself as independent as he possibly could be. He'd emotionally distanced himself from his siblings and, really, it was better that way. Distance allowed a buffer against the hurt that emotional connections always created. Distance allowed him to keep control.

He'd come close to losing control once and he'd paid the price for it. Over two months and on a continent across the world, Cady had snuck under his skin and into his heart and he'd lost himself in her.

She was just a young man's stupidity, Beck told himself for the millionth time. Every guy had that one woman he idolized in his head. It didn't mean anything.

He'd been trying for nearly a decade to believe his own BS. At the time she'd meant *everything*.

"Where are you this time?" Amy demanded, pulling him out of his thoughts. "Please, please tell me you're lying on a beach somewhere reading a book."

Not his style. Admittedly, all his breaks were action based and full of physical activity, but at least his brain slowed down from constantly operating at warp speed.

"Saariselkä, Finland."

"Of course you are. Heli-skiing?"

Beck smiled at her concern. Amy hated it when he indulged in his love for high-risk adventure sports. "Not this time. Cross-country skiing."

"Dangerous?"

"Not at all," Beck lied. There had been a couple of hairy traverses this morning, but he was here in one piece, wasn't he? What was the point of upsetting her?

"Liar."

Beck smiled and took a sip of his beer. Since meeting Amy in Thailand, she'd been his closest friend. He was reasonably sociable but the reserve he cultivated meant that he didn't have many close friends. Amy had ignored his "keep out" signs and had barged her way into his life. He'd flown to Hanoi after saying goodbye to Cady in Bangkok and Amy had immediately sensed that he was hurting. She'd plastered herself to his side and traveled with him as he hauled his dented heart over the soil of various Southeast Asian countries.

You couldn't BS a person who'd witnessed your heart bleed.

Amy had been a kind and consistent presence, a

true friend. And because of her sexual orientation, they'd never complicated their friendship with sex. He and Amy had quit traveling at the same time and he'd joined Ballantyne International, knowing that it was time to put his MBA to work. Amy had needed a job and he'd arranged for her to do some temporary secretarial work at Ballantyne International. Within three months, she'd made herself indispensable, not only to him, but also to his ex-guardian and uncle, Connor Ballantyne. Amy, irreverent and hip but brutally efficient, became Connor's eyes, ears and right hand and she'd been devastated when Connor was diagnosed with Alzheimer's.

It was Amy who'd made all the arrangements to transport Jaeger back home when he was involved in that car accident in Italy, and Amy who'd held Beckett's hand at his brother's hospital bed and at his uncle's funeral.

"So, what's happening at work?" Beckett asked her, tapping his finger against the neck of his cold beer bottle.

"The usual. I sent out the briefs to various PR firms today to bid for the rebranding strategy."

A small frown appeared between Beck's eyes. "Which firms did you send the brief to?"

Amy named a few firms Beck was familiar with and he nodded his approval. "Linc instructed me to send them to smaller firms, too, ones that think outside the box," Amy added.

"Hard to find."

"Jules had a suggestion or two."

"Who?"

Amy shrugged. "You wouldn't know them."

Beck couldn't identify the emotion flashing in Amy's eyes and he frowned at her uncharacteristic reticence.

"Well, let's see what they come up with. Email me their bid documents and I can go through them."

Amy shook her head. "Linc told me that that he'll run through them and pick the top four to do detailed presentations. You'll be back for their presentations, so you can weigh in then."

Amy had her stubborn face on and he knew he'd lost this round. To be honest, he really didn't want to plow through the bid documents. It was tedious work and if Linc wanted to do it, he'd let him.

"Listen, Beck…"

Amy bit the inside of her lip and Beck knew she was about to say something he didn't want to hear. Worse, she had the same look on her face when every year or so she suggested that he track down Cady, that he see where she was and what she was doing. That he find a real connection, like the one she and Julia had.

And every year he told her he wasn't interested, that he was perfectly happy as he was. Well, not happy, but content.

"Guess who I saw today?" Amy asked before he could tell her not to go there.

Beck tensed. He didn't need her to say the name; he heard it in her voice. "Where?"

"At Bonnets, a cocktail bar off—"

"I know it." Beck felt hot then cold. He stared down at the patterned comforter, the blue-and-white pattern rising and falling.

He forced his tongue to move. "New York is in so many ways a small town. Listen, I have to go."

"No, you don't. You're just trying to avoid talking about Cady. I need to tell you—"

"Bye, Ames, I'll talk to you soon." Beck slapped his laptop shut on her annoyed squeal.

He ran his hand through his wavy hair and flipped the laptop open again. He quickly accessed a file, opening the one photo he'd kept of her. She was lying on the sand at Maya Bay on Phi Phi island, her bright pink bikini a blaze of triangles against her tanned skin. She'd turned her head to look at him and her long and silky hair dropped into the sand. Her startling eyes brimmed with laughter. And love.

They'd been apart for nearly ten years and would be apart for a lifetime more. He knew that, accepted that. That was why he never thought about her, said her name, discussed those first few months of his trip. They were completely, solidly over. So why was he looking at a photo of her, wishing that things had turned out differently?

Because he wasn't busy and he had time to think. And to remember.

But mostly because he was, despite his high IQ, a moron.

Two

Beck exited the private elevator that only he, his siblings and Amy had access to and stepped into the corridor of Ballantyne International. The corporate offices were situated above their flagship, and oldest, jewelry store on Fifth Avenue. Unlike the classic decor of the store below, the Ballantyne offices were light, airy and modern. Beck, as director of finance and the group's troubleshooter, saw an intern walking down the hall to the copy room and struggled to remember his name.

"Cole, Cody..."

The kid turned and offered a tentative smile. "Charles, sir."

He had the *C* right and he was only in his early thirties, far too young to be called sir. Beck shrugged out of his leather jacket and laid it across the top of his suitcase and pushed the bag in the intern's direction. "Put this in Amy's office and bring me a very large cup of coffee. I'll be in Linc's office until further notice."

"Mr. Ballantyne—Linc—is in the boardroom with the other Mr. Ballantyne and Ms. Ballantyne."

Beck nodded, holding back his smile at the mouthful of *B*s. "Thanks." He turned and headed in the opposite direction, greeting the odd person he encountered on his way. Monday morning and thanks to his flight being diverted to Newark because of an anticipated emergency landing at La Guardia, he was late. He'd picked the least aggressive cab driver in the city and his trip from New Jersey had taken forever. He hated being late.

Beck opened the door to the conference room and pushed his shirtsleeves up his elbows. As Charles said, his siblings were all in the room, but Amy wasn't.

"Driven is back," Jaeger stated, leaning back in his chair.

Jaeger had given him the nickname shortly after his thirteenth birthday when he graduated at the top of his class and made both the state swimming and track teams. They thought that he was an outlier, one of those kids who was gifted in both sports and academics. They never suspected that he'd always felt the need to prove himself worthy of being born a Ballantyne.

"How was Finland?" Linc asked, standing up to

give him a one-arm hug. Linc was almost as big as he was and a couple of years older. Beck stepped away and bent down to drop a kiss in Sage's black hair. Like him, his brothers were big and brawny but Sage had the body of a ballerina.

"Good," Beck replied, slapping his palm against Jaeger's. "How's Ty? Flu gone?"

Jaeger nodded. "He's fine. When are you going to find a woman and bake yourself a kid, Beck? They are a blast."

Oh, no, not this again. Beck noticed the glint of mischief that appeared in Jaeger's eyes and did an internal eye roll. Since reconnecting and falling in love with Piper, Jaeger was determined to pull his siblings into his sparkly, loved-up world. Beckett had no objection to being loved up; he just didn't need the emotional connection. He had no intention of flirting with that hell again. After Cady, it had taken him six months to feel halfway human and another six before he'd felt relatively whole again.

He refused to think of her, not now, not ever. He hadn't been able to discuss her with Amy; couldn't bear to even hear her name.

"I've had a nightmare morning so don't start," Beck said as a hesitant tap came from the half open door. He pulled the door open, took his cup of coffee from Charles, said thanks and took a reviving sip. "So, this looks like a meeting. What's on the agenda?"

"Only one thing," Linc told him.

"And that is?"

"Deciding who we are going to appoint to oversee our new PR and rebranding campaign."

Linc dropped into the chair at the head of the conference table and Beck sat to his right. "A lot has happened lately. At the beginning of last week, I met with eight PR companies, including Jenkins and Pale, who's always done our PR and advertising."

As the Ballantyne finance director and all round troubleshooter, this item for discussion was in Beck's wheelhouse. Jaeger sourced magnificent gems and Sage was their head designer, but Beck and Linc ran the business side of Ballantyne International.

"We decided that we needed to rebrand a while back, but I moved it higher up our priority list," Linc said. "As we know, Connor was the face of Ballantyne. He had the personal connections and brought charisma to the brand. Without him the Ballantyne brand is...staid, stuffy."

Linc leaned forward, clasping his hands on the table and looking at Beck. "The day you left town Sheik Abdul Ameen went to Moreau's and bought a diamond bracelet for his mother instead of coming to us. I did a sales audit and I noticed that other long-term, super-rich clients have also moved on."

Their clients' loyalty was to Connor, not to them, Beck realized.

"But we have the same quality of gems we always have had," Sage protested.

"Yeah, but we don't have Connor selling them," Linc pointed out. "Connor knew his clients inside out. They liked dealing with him and only with him."

"And our younger, rich clients want sexy and they want hip." Beck sipped his coffee, agreeing with his brother. Linc was brilliant at managing their staff and dealing with their shareholders. He was a hands-on manager, but Beckett was their strategist, able to see the big picture. He and Linc worked really well together with each of them playing to their strengths.

He looked back to Linc. "So you met with these PR firms and…?"

"And I isolated four who, I think, have some idea of what we want. They aren't perfect by any means, but their ideas have potential. One of them is better than the others."

"Who?" Sage asked Linc.

Linc shook his head. "Listen to their pitches and make up your own mind."

Beck glanced at his watch. "When are we due to start?"

"Fifteen minutes," Jaeger replied.

"Good, I have time to change. Where's Amy?" Beck asked, standing up, his coffee cup in his hand.

"She should be out in the reception area meeting and greeting the company representatives," Linc replied.

Beck nodded. "I just need to say hi to her and I'll see you back here in fifteen."

"Beckett," Linc said as he reached the conference door. Beck heard the note of concern in Linc's voice and turned around to look at his brother.

"Yeah?"

"Remember that we're making the right choice

for the company. That might not be the right choice for you."

Beck looked from Linc to Jaeger and to Sage's worried eyes. "What the hell do you mean by that?" he demanded.

"You'll see."

Beck heard Linc's ominous words and felt a shiver run up his spine. He looked down the hall to the bank of elevators and wondered why he had the instinctive urge to run.

What in the name of all that was holy was she doing here?

Saving her business, Cady reminded herself. No more, no less. Sitting on one of the low, tangerine-colored ottomans in the reception area of Ballantyne and Company, she placed her hands under her thighs and ordered her knees to stop knocking. God, there was Gayle from Jenkins and Pale, Ballantyne's long-term PR partner. And was she talking to Matthew from Anchor and Chain Consulting? They were at the top of the PR food chain. She was plankton. Or the stuff plankton ate.

Cady fixed her eyes on the large, abstract painting on the wall behind the receptionist's head and begged her queasy stomach to settle down. *Yes, baby, it's been a hell of a week, but I had no choice. If we want to eat and have a roof over our heads, I have to work and not sleep, as I so want to do.*

Ten days ago, after her disastrous meeting with Tom, she'd doubted she could pull herself out of this hole. Accepting that her baby's father was a cyanide pill, she'd headed back to the office that night, knowing that she had plans to make. When dawn broke that Saturday morning, she realized that she had three months to turn her business around. If she didn't she would be single, pregnant and broke.

Not knowing how to do that, she'd fallen asleep on the sofa in her office and was jerked awake later that morning by the ping of her computer, informing her of a new email. Congenitally unable to ignore a communication, whether it was an email, a text message or a smoke signal, Cady opened the email from pr@ballantynes.com.

Ballantyne International is seeking to appoint a specialist PR agency to work with us to reinvent our century-old brand. We require a passionate and creative firm/individual to develop and install a range of external communications and media activities.

The brief attached sets out our objectives and requirements, together with a range of background information on Ballantyne International. Interested agencies are asked to respond in full by 9:00 a.m. Monday January 3 at the latest.

Somehow, somewhere, the PR person at Ballantyne's had heard of her and she was invited to the party. Late, but still invited.

Given the choice, she would've avoided doing work for Beck's company but she didn't have that luxury. Winning this project would keep Collins

Consulting afloat. Sure, she was a minnow competing with the sharks and she didn't have that much of a chance, but if she didn't submit a proposal she didn't have a chance at all.

Basically, it was a choice between telling her parents she was pregnant, single and could support herself and her child or that she was pregnant, single and could they help her out until she found a job?

Yeah, when she broke it down like that, it was no contest.

But first, she needed to face Beck.

At the thought of him, she resisted the urge to grab her laptop and run. She had no other option. She had a business to save, a baby to raise, money to earn. Unlike Beck, she didn't have endless family money and hefty trusts as a backup plan.

Not fair, she chided herself. Beck never used his position as a Ballantyne heir as an excuse not to achieve. If anything, it spurred him on to prove to the world that he would be successful whether he was a Ballantyne or not. Even though the Ballantynes were practically American royalty, Ivy League schools didn't hand out MBAs just because you were rich.

But she didn't want to be fair. Beck's actions in Thailand, his playing loose and fast with her feelings and her love, had devastated her. And she wished more than anything there was something she could do to never lay eyes on him again.

"Cady?"

At the sound of her name Cady looked up and saw Amy standing over her. Amy? *Beck's Amy?*

"Hi. I'm glad you made it through the selection process." Amy smiled at her, effortlessly confident.

Cady quickly realized Amy must have sent her the pitch documents and the brief; the timing made sense since she'd given her card to Julia Parker on Friday night and she received the email on Saturday morning. Well, the how made sense but not the why.

"You emailed me," Cady said as she stood up. "Why?"

"Take a walk with me," Amy suggested and Cady fell into step with her as she proceeded down the hallway that led to the glass-walled offices of Ballantyne International.

Amy stopped under another large, expensive art piece. "Linc asked me to contact a range of PR firms, both big and small, to bid for this job. Julia said that you did good work for Trott's, so I gave you a chance to pitch, just like I gave seven other companies the same chance. Linc liked your ideas and you're one of the final four."

"So this has nothing to do with you feeling guilty about taking my place with Beck?"

Cady felt like a twit the second her words left her mouth, and Amy's laughter deepened her embarrassment. God, she sounded like a sulky teenager.

When she stopped laughing at her, Amy said, "That's the funniest thing I've heard for a long, long time."

"Hey, Ames."

Oh, damn. She recognized that voice; she heard it

in her dreams often enough. Dark as sin, rich as butter, warm as hot chocolate after playing in the snow.

Cady looked over Amy's shoulder and watched him walk down the hall toward them, dressed in battered jeans, boots and a navy, long-sleeved T-shirt the exact color of his eyes. The shirt was tight across his chest, skimming his muscled stomach. Blond stubble covered his cheeks, and his wavy hair brushed his collar. He looked rough and hot and fifty times better-looking than the Greek god she'd traveled with so many years ago.

His hair was a lot shorter than she remembered; the man bun was gone and so was the heavy beard. His eyes, a brilliant dark blue, seemed harder and his face thinner. His mouth, that clever mouth that had once dropped hot kisses all over her body, was a slash in his face. He looked hard and tough and every inch the smart, determined, sometimes ruthless businessman he was reputed to be. He looked like he could handle any and all trouble that came his way.

Her knees buckled and air rushed out of her lungs as she remembered those brawny arms around her, the way he used to easily lift her off her feet to kiss him. Cady tasted him on her tongue, could feel his heat, and smell his citrus and cedar scent. She was back in Thailand, the air was muggy, the sky was blue and she was turned on.

Breath short, mouth dry, panties damp...so turned on.

Oh, dammit!

Beck didn't pay her any attention as he scooped

Amy off her feet and dropped a kiss on her lips. He hugged her again before he allowed her feet to hit the ground, his hands on her hips.

"Before you ask, no, I didn't bring you a present," he told Amy, that open smile flipping Cady's stomach up and over. She shivered, remembering the sexy phrases he'd muttered in that same baritone as he'd taught her how to give and receive physical pleasure.

Amy mock pouted before half turning away from him. Cady saw her suck in a deep breath before she placed her hand on Cady's bicep. "Obviously you remember Cady, Beck."

Color drained from Beck's face as he looked from Cady to Amy and back again. The warmth in his eyes faded and she watched, fascinated, as his eyes raked her from head to toe. She saw his eyes deepen with… God, could that be desire? But when they met hers again, they were the dark, cold blue of a winter's ocean.

"Cady. What are you doing here?" His voice held no emotion as his words whipped across her.

Before she could answer, Amy flashed him a bright smile. "Cady is in PR. Julia knows Cady's work and she suggested that Cady take a stab at developing a proposal to rebrand Ballantyne's. Since Julia is one of the most respected consultants in the city and since she rarely makes recommendations, I thought her advice was worth taking."

Beck didn't drop his eyes from hers as he leaned one big shoulder into the wall. God, he was still so sexy—no, scrap that. He was even hotter than he used to be. And so remote, disinterested.

His eyes finally moved to Amy and as he narrowed them on her, Cady realized that he was pissed.

So Beck wasn't happy to see her.

She couldn't do this; she absolutely could not be around him. He'd sent her home, tossed her away. She couldn't stay here and be constantly reminded that she wasn't enough.

Cady started to turn to walk away and then she remembered what was at stake. Her business was her only source of income and she needed that income. If she wasn't pregnant, she would leave but she was now responsible for another life, and walking away wasn't that simple anymore.

She needed this damned job.

Cady planted her feet and turned her attention back to her ex-lover and potential client and to Amy, who obviously had an important position in his company.

"Linc asked me to source proposals from new, hungry firms as well as the established companies we've worked with before. Cady made it through the first round and she's about to do her presentation," Amy explained, still sounding cool and composed.

Cady could see the tension in his body, see his fist clench. "You've gone too far, Amy."

"I have not. This is a business arrangement, a job. She's creative, hungry and needs work, and Ballantyne's needs someone creative, something different. You're making this personal, not me," Amy retorted.

How could it not be? What they had had been very personal indeed. She allowed this man to do things to her that still made her blush. And she'd returned the favor...

As she remembered hot mouths, desperate hands, labored breathing and mind-shattering orgasms, she had to place her hand on the wall to keep her balance. Beck's eyes slammed into hers and she caught a flash of awareness, a lick of fiery heat, and she knew that he knew exactly what she was thinking. For an instant he was there with her, holding himself above her, about to slide into her.

His eyes always turned that particular shade of cobalt-blue when he was turned on. Cady licked her lips and dropped her eyes to his crotch...

Nope, nothing. No action at all. Mortified, she lifted her hot face to see the ice in his eyes. So, she was alone in that little fantasy, and Beck was definitely not taking a walk down memory lane.

But Beck was giving her another once-over, his gaze starting at her nude heels, moving slowly up her skinny black trousers to her blush-pink silk blouse. She'd pulled her long hair into a severe braid, which she twisted into a low knot at the back of her head, and her makeup, while minimalist, was flawless. With black, heavy-framed glasses, she looked every inch the New York businesswoman and nothing like the free-spirited girl he used to know.

While he inspected her like she was a car he was considering buying, she thought that Beck was now bigger and broader, harder, and he exuded power from every sexy pore. Even dressed casually, he emitted a don't-mess-with-me vibe that dried up the moisture in her mouth and sent it straight to that special spot between her legs.

Damn.

Amy broke the tension by poking Beck with her red-tipped finger. "You need to change. You can't listen to presentations looking like you've just walked off a trail."

Beck grabbed her finger and held it, just enough for Amy's eyes to widen and for her to realize that Beck was still pissed off. "Do try to remember who the boss is."

Amy, utterly indefatigable, just grinned. "I do. It's me. Let's get back to work, people."

Cady spun around and walked back to the reception area and ignored the curious looks she received from her fellow competitors. Beck, she presumed, went to clean up.

Neither of them saw the gleeful expression on Amy's face or heard her whispered words. "Watching them is going to be so much fun."

Three

Keyed up and tense after her ninety-minute-long presentation, Cady left the conference room feeling like a washed-out rag. Needing a comfort break, she headed down the hall to the ladies' room, thinking that she'd wash her hands and face, reapply some war paint and try to catch her breath. The Ballantyne siblings—with the exception of Beck, who had just sat there, as immovable and silent as a rock— had bombarded her with questions, most of which she'd deftly answered.

She'd done her best in the limited time she'd had, putting together a mammoth strategy for a global company, but she had no illusions. She was up against the best in the business. If she got the contract then she'd earn herself a get-out-of-bankruptcy card. If she didn't, in a month or two she'd be packing her bags and throwing herself on the mercy of her parents.

They'd take her in; there was no doubt about it. But she'd have to learn to live with disapproving looks and the what-were-you-thinking lectures. And the image of the perfect family, the one her mother tried so hard to project, would be shattered. The pastor's daughter, single and pregnant, the one who had so much potential, would be hot, hot gossip.

Her mother was going to *kill* her.

Cady felt a big hand wrap around her upper bicep and she spun around to look into Beckett's deep blue eyes, the exact color of the navy-and-white polka-dot tie he now wore over a finely striped light-blue-and-white shirt. Walking into the conference room earlier, the last company to present, she'd immediately noticed that he'd changed and couldn't help thinking he should always wear blue. The cuffs of his shirt were folded over the sleeves of his trendy cardigan, and both sleeves were pushed up to his elbows, showing his thick, muscled forearms.

Beckett was a snappy dresser.

"Beckett, I need to use the facilities," she protested as he walked her past the ladies' room.

"I have a private bathroom adjoining my office," he growled and Cady had to half jog to keep up with his long-legged stride. He ignored Amy's startled face as he walked past her desk and into the office on the right. Through the glass walls, a feature of the Ballantyne offices, she could see that Linc's office was empty. Cady wondered if they ever felt like they were working in a fish tank.

Beck pushed her through the glass door into his messy office.

"The bathroom is through there." He nodded to a door at the other end of the large space. "When you're done, we're going to talk."

That didn't sound good. Cady kept her face blank, not wanting Beck to see her flinch. Nodding once, she placed her laptop bag on one of the two bucket chairs facing his ridiculously large desk and headed for the bathroom.

After using the facilities, she took her time washing her hands and touching up her makeup. Beckett could wait until she got her galloping heart under control.

Cady gripped the counter of the vanity and stared at herself in the mirror. Severe hair, white face, bands of blue under her unusual eyes. Two stripes of color on each cheekbone, saving her from the need to apply blush.

She looked like what she was: a stressed-out woman trying to hustle a job. She didn't look pregnant but she did look flustered, and a little unhinged. She was older and more experienced, so why did she feel like she was nineteen again? Her palms were damp, her panties, too. He just needed to touch her and she'd go up in flames.

She might be older, but she wasn't any wiser, Cady thought, washing her hands for the second time.

"You're stalling, Cady. Get out here. I don't have all day."

"Yes, Your Lordship," Cady muttered, yanking the door open and stepping back into his office.

Beck stood by the floor-to-ceiling windows, his hands jammed into his pockets, every square inch of his long body taut with tension. Cady walked over to the window and stopped next to him, her arms folded across her chest. She felt equally uptight herself.

Cady looked down to the iconic Manhattan street below and watched the pedestrians navigate the busy intersection, their chins and noses tucked into scarves or coat collars, their faces ruddy from the icy winter wind.

"Why are you doing this, Cady?"

She turned to look at him. This was, at least, a question she could answer.

"It's my job, Beckett. Like you, but on a far smaller scale, I am running a business, a business that I'd prefer not to see go under. I need new, bigger clients. Ballantyne International is a new, big client." Cady shrugged, knowing that her edgy attitude wasn't conducive to good client–service provider relationships.

Beckett rolled his head on his shoulders and rubbed the back of his neck. "I would've liked some damn warning that you were going to drop back into my life."

Why? She didn't mean anything to him. He'd broken up with her by sending her home. He'd gone on to Vietnam, hooked up with Amy there and then God knew where. She was the one who had the right to feel caught off guard. Then again, she had had days to prepare herself to see him again. He'd only had a few minutes.

But since she meant nothing to him, why should it matter?

"This is just business, Beckett. I was a teenager and that was a lifetime ago. I have real problems to worry about—" like pregnancy and poverty "—and I really don't have the time or the energy to spend thinking about something that lasted a millisecond a million years ago."

She needed this contract and that meant putting her and Beckett on a very firm this-is-business footing. A cynical smile touched the corner of his mouth as his eyes dropped from hers to her mouth and back again.

"Are you really trying to tell me that the chemistry between us has disappeared? That you weren't remembering Thailand, hot nights and sweaty bodies? The way I'd kiss you?" His eyes dropped to her crotch, and Cady thought her panties might burst into flames. "How it felt when I sank into you?"

So he had been with her earlier, thinking of the way they'd made love to each other. She had seen the desire in his eyes and it wasn't her imagination.

Right now if she took one step she'd be up against his hard chest. If she pushed herself onto her toes, she could touch her lips to his.

God, she wanted to kiss him, touch the hard muscles she'd once known so well.

Job. Money. Contract. Baby. Glass walls.

The words cut through her haze of lust and she remembered why she was here and what was at stake. Cady sucked in a breath, tossed her head back, lifted her chin and borrowed her mother's you're-on-the-path-to-hell look. "We're going to go there, *really*?"

"Yeah, really."

Beckett slapped his hand on a switch panel and the glass walls turned opaque and Amy, and her curious face, disappeared.

Cady had to smile. "Now that's a cool trick."

"I think so."

Beckett stepped into her personal space and Cady's folded arms brushed his rock-hard abdomen. Her heart bounced off her rib cage, and her stomach felt like it was taking a roller-coaster ride, but she'd be damned if she'd let Beck see how much his hot and hard body affected her.

Beck smiled, lifted a hand and rested the tip of his index finger in the V of her throat. "Your pulse is trying to burst through your skin."

Damned pulse. *Heart, stop beating,* she ordered.

Beck's hot fingertip ran up the side of her throat until he reached her jaw. "God, your eyes. My memory didn't do them justice. Silver and green all contained in a ring of emerald."

Cady swallowed and shook her head. "Don't do this, Beckett."

"I think I have to," he replied, the heat of his hand scalding her jaw. His other hand grasped her hip and he pulled her into him.

Cady tried to keep her arms folded, she really did, so she had no idea how her hands ended up being splayed onto his chest. And why was she tipping her head up, watching his mouth as it slowly descended to hers?

Beck's lips were pure magic, Cady thought, as his mouth took possession of hers. She felt his hand cup her right butt cheek and pull her up into his hard body. She closed her eyes, not quite believing that he was holding her, that his mouth was on hers. It felt like it belonged there, as if she'd been created to be kissed by him. Beck kissed her like he owned her, like she was still his. He kissed her with unreserved passion, unafraid to show her how turned on he was. His mouth, lips, tongue…all hot, silky, sexy.

Underneath the fabric of her trousers, Cady felt the heat of his fingers pushing into her skin and she wished that he would use his hands to do something interesting. Touching her breasts and swiping his thumb over her nipple sounded like a really good idea right then. But Beck did neither. He continued to kiss her, his tongue tangling with hers until she didn't know where she started or he ended.

The strident ring of her phone in the side pocket of her tote bag had Beck pulling away from her. He cocked his head and nodded at her bag. "Want to get that?"

Cady couldn't form any words so she just shook her head, her hands gripping his clothing to pull him back to her. She needed more kisses, more of him… It had been so damn long.

"Just business, huh?"

Beck's sarcastic comment had her eyes flying open and she immediately noticed the sarcastic glint in his eyes, the muscle ticking in his jaw. Cady released her grip and took a decisive step back. "Was that a test?" she demanded, annoyed to hear the shake in her voice.

"Sure. And we failed." Under his shirt Beck's biceps bunched as he folded his arms and widened his stance. He looked big and tough and intimidating, but Cady knew that he was as deeply affected by that kiss as she was. It was cold comfort.

"I don't mix business with pleasure, Cady," Beck told her, his tone non-negotiable. "And I will do anything and everything to protect Ballantyne's."

"I'm working with you and not against you, Beck," Cady protested.

"This rebranding strategy is the most important marketing project of the last twenty years and I do not want my business performance affected because we can't keep our hands off each other."

"We're adults, Beckett. If we decide to keep it professional, we can," Cady told him.

Pfft, her inner voice mocked. *Just like you did with Tom? What a liar!*

"It always blows up and we're pretty combustible as it is," Beck stated.

Cady released a frustrated sigh and at her sides, her hands pulled up into fists. *Do not react, do not react.* "It's unlike you to put the cart before the horse,

Beckett. Why don't we see if I am awarded the contract first? I have some pretty strong competition."

Beck sent her a long, hard look. "I'll give you twenty thousand dollars if you walk out that door and forget all about us, and Ballantyne's."

Cady felt her knees buckle and she dropped down to sit on the edge of his visitor's chair, unaware that she was sharing the space with her laptop bag. "Sorry... *What?*"

"I'll pay you twenty K for you not to take this contract."

That was what she thought he said. Cady lifted her head to look at Beck, conscious of a throbbing pain underneath her rib cage. Were those three months in Thailand such a bad memory that he couldn't stand to be around her, couldn't wrap his head around working with her? Okay, she hadn't loved traveling, mostly because her parents had been so dead set against the notion. She'd been pulled in two directions by her parents and by Beck, but they'd had some fun. Hadn't they?

Cady didn't understand any of this and her first impulse was to tell him to take his offer and stick it. She opened her mouth to blast him and then she remembered that this wasn't just about her. She had a child on the way and if she refused his offer, and wasn't awarded the contract, she'd be broke and soon homeless. If she took the money, she'd buy herself a hell of a lot of breathing room.

First prize would be landing the contract, of course, then all her money hassles would be solved.

"Well?"

It was tempting to take the cash and run. She opened her mouth to agree, struggling to think past the feelings of inadequacy and confusion. But if she took his money she'd be dancing to someone else's tune, to Beck's little ditty. He'd be putting her on a metaphorical plane again and sending her away because once again she was inconvenient.

She'd done that once and it took years for her to patch her heart back together, to regain her confidence.

She'd be running away, taking the easy option.

Have faith in yourself, Cady. If you don't get this project, you'll make another plan.

Beck no longer had the power to dictate her actions. She wasn't a teenager anymore.

Cady stood up, straightened her spine and sent him a death stare. "That's not going to happen, Beckett. I either get the contract or I don't. That's business and that's life. If I do get it, you're just going to have to deal with whatever problem you still have with me. If I don't, I will sort myself out. I've done okay on my own for a long time and I don't need you or your money."

Cady picked up her laptop bag, slung it over her shoulder and grabbed the strap of her tote bag. "I think we're done here."

Cady walked to the door and placed her hand on the doorknob. She looked at Beck, still standing at his desk, his eyes on her. "My pride and my self-respect are not for sale, Ballantyne."

* * *

Cady left the door open behind her and because Beck didn't want to see or speak to anyone for, oh, a hundred years, he hurried to the door and slammed it shut. He banged his head against the jamb, wishing he had a punching bag to plow his fist into.

From the moment he met her, Cady had the ability to turn his life upside down and inside out. And when she was awarded this PR contract—and she would be, since her presentation and strategy were creative, innovative and interesting—he wouldn't be able to avoid her.

Damn. He liked his life as it was. Drama free.

He also liked the fact that he was firmly in control of it. Since Connor was no longer here to hound him about being unemotional, to demand that he open up and communicate, he was able to stay on the fringes of the family group, present and supportive but not emotionally engaged.

He loved his family, intensely, but he still felt that deep down his siblings blamed him for his parents' deaths and if they didn't, then they should.

If he hadn't begged them to return home…

Feeling responsible and unable to rectify the problem, he'd realized that the only way to redeem himself was to show them that he was worthy of being a Ballantyne. At eight years old, under a table at the post-funeral reception, his drive and ambition were born.

The only time he'd taken a break from feeling responsible, from feeling like he had to prove his worth, was when he was traveling with Cady. Despite her family issues, he'd relaxed around her, and the freedom to be himself was intoxicating. She didn't care that he received his MBA when he was twenty, that he'd been a nationally ranked swimmer, that he was an heir to the Ballantyne fortune. To Cady, he was just Beck and he'd loved being just Beck.

He acknowledged that was the real reason he sent her away. For years he'd justified his actions by reminding himself that she was miserable, but in truth, the longer he spent with her, the less important his ambition and drive became. What Cady thought or believed about him started to become more important than what he believed about himself, and he couldn't have that.

Years later their attraction burned hotter and brighter than before—just being in the same room as her set his nerve endings on fire—and Beck worried that, if she stuck around and if he spent any time with her at all, history would repeat itself.

He had an obligation to his family, to Ballantyne's, to help Linc steer this mammoth ship of a business in a global economy. Ballantyne International, and all its many subsidiaries, including the high-end jewelry stores that were the face of the business, were his top and only priority, and he had to guard against anything that threatened his duty to Ballantyne's.

Cady had, and if he wasn't careful, she might again. He couldn't take the chance.

Beck lifted his head off the doorjamb and as he did so, the door flew open and smacked him in the forehead. He groaned and stepped back, placing his hand over his forehead.

"Why the hell are you standing behind the door?" Linc asked, unsympathetic.

"Crap! Why didn't you knock?" Beck demanded, dropping his hand to check for blood.

"Problems," Linc said, stepping inside and closing the door behind him.

"It's been that type of day," Beck said, walking back to his desk, conscious of his throbbing head. He dropped into his leather chair and placed his ankle on his opposite knee. "What's up?"

Linc paced the area in front of Beck's desk. If there was one good thing to come out of his parents' deaths, then it was Linc, and his mother, Jo. Unable to cope with three kids, Connor hired Jo as his housekeeper and nanny, and she and her son moved into the brownstone with the rest of them. A few years later, Connor formally adopted his nephews and niece, and also Linc, thereby legalizing their emotional bond. As he had been then, Linc was still the person they ran to when their wheels fell off.

He was their brother, not by blood, but by choice.

Linc placed his hands on Beck's desk, his gray eyes worried. "So, Tate Harper just called me."

Now there was a name he hadn't heard for a while. "Harper? Kari's sister?"

Linc nodded, anger flashing in his eyes. Beck didn't blame him. When their son, Shaw, was six weeks old, Kari up and left Linc and their son. After another two months, Linc's PI friend tracked her to

Austin. Reame returned with a message from Kari telling Linc that she wasn't coming back and a document signing over full custody of Shaw to Linc.

Kari's sister, a travel presenter, seemed as flaky as her sister.

"What does she want?" Beck asked.

"She has something urgent to discuss with me." Linc shrugged. "No idea what but, knowing the Harper sisters, it can't be anything good."

"Have you met her?"

"No."

"If she's anything like Kari then she'll be very easy on the eyes," Beck stated.

"And, if she's anything like her sister, as cracked as a sidewalk," Linc said, looking and sounding tense. "We're meeting in an hour, at the brownstone."

"It's that important that it can't wait until the end of the day?" Beck asked, surprised. Like him, Linc was rarely distracted from his work at Ballantyne's.

"So she says. Kari probably sent her to try to sweet-talk me into sending her some cash," Linc said, sounding bitter.

"Just say no, dude." Beck dropped his foot and looked at the piles of paper on his desk. A quick glance at his monitor showed that he had a slew of emails he needed to look at. Taking a break was good for him, but the recuperative effects were quickly negated by the avalanche of work that hit his desk in his absence.

Linc started to leave, then he turned back around

to Beck. "We need to make a decision about the PR consultant."

Beckett tensed. He prayed they'd choose someone else, anyone else, just not Cady. Was he allowed, just this one time, to put his interests above those of Ballantyne's?

"The three of us want to hire Cady."

Of course they did.

"Can you live with that? Jaeger says that you can, that whatever happened between you and Cady occurred a long time ago and that you're adults now and not kids. Sage isn't so sure."

Sage was a wise woman.

What was he supposed to say? No, don't hire her because she threatens my calm, controlled world? He'd rather bang a rock against his head than admit to that.

"Sure, we're adults. Anyway, I'm not going to deal with her, Carol is. She's our in-house PR person."

Linc pulled a face and Beck's stomach dipped and flipped.

"Carol's asked for a three-month sabbatical. Her father is terminally ill and she needs some time to be with him. I thought that, with a new PR person coming in, she could take that time." Linc perched on the edge of Beck's desk and tapped his finger against the frame of the photograph of Connor and his adopted kids. "I need you to work with Cady and be her go-to person within Ballantyne's."

Oh, hell, no. "Ah, come on, Linc! Are you trying to torture me?"

Linc smiled. "Not deliberately, but torturing you is always a pleasure." His face turned serious. "You understand best of all what we need in terms of this rebranding strategy because you have the type of brain that sees the big picture. You also know more of the family history than any of us. Besides, Jaeger is leaving for Thailand on a buying trip, and Sage is heading to Hong Kong for a jewelry show. And I have my own fires to put out."

Something in his brother's voice caught his attention and Beck frowned. "Like?"

Linc stood up and shoved his hands into the pockets of his suit pants. "I've been hearing rumors about someone buying up massive blocks of Ballantyne International stock."

Beck rubbed the back of his neck. "It can't be a hostile takeover. The four of us own controlling shares so we'll never lose the company."

"Yeah, but why would someone want so many shares? I want to know who's behind this and why."

"Don't you think it makes better sense for me, as finance director, to do that and you deal with Cady?"

Linc shook his head. "I have a better relationship with the shareholders than you do."

That was true. Beckett scowled at his brother. "Do I have a choice about working with Cady?"

Linc grinned. "No."

Crap. There went his calm, controlled life.

"Just try to keep your hands off her, Beck. Or, if you can't, keep it tidy until you're out of the office, dude."

Beck sent him a hard look. "You should know better than to accuse me of that."

Linc raised his eyebrows. "Then, I'm really interested—and not just a little worried—as to why you've decided to start wearing lipstick. And, FYI, that shade of pink isn't your color."

Busted.

Four

Two weeks later, Cady checked her email for the final time that night and reluctantly tapped the red X to close the program. For the last two weeks she'd done market research and before she moved on to the next phase of the project, she needed to speak to Beck. His lack of response meant that she had the weekend free. The thought of not working over the weekend made her feel twitchy. At least when she was working she didn't have time to think of him and remember that kiss.

Cady walked past her wine rack on the way to her kitchen—wishing she could indulge in a glass or three—and opened her fridge to remove a carton of fruit juice. It was Friday night, she was alone and pregnant, wearing an old pair of yoga pants, thick socks and a long T-shirt of Tom's he'd failed to reclaim.

He'd taken everything else when he visited her a week ago—his CDs, the ceramic kitchen knives he'd given her for her last birthday, the abstract painting of red and yellow globs she'd never liked. While he'd been gathering his possessions, he'd intimated that he'd be prepared to resume their relationship if and when she freed herself of her "responsibilities."

He might even throw some business her way.

Since she didn't have the slightest intention of either aborting her baby or talking to him again, Cady marched to the door, opened it and told him to get out. She'd considered yanking one of the ceramic knives from its holder and stabbing him, but she didn't want to waste the little money she had on bail.

Cady sipped her juice, walked over to her kitchen window and stared at the street below. The sleet-tinged rain fell steadily and the streets were deserted. Loneliness, cold and heavy, fell over her and she wished that she could pick up the phone and call someone. Anyone. Building her business had taken all her time, and the few friends she'd had slipped away. Then Tom came into her life and she'd convinced herself that she wasn't lonely, that someone with a lover and a business couldn't be lonely.

But she had been. She was.

She wished she had one good friend she could call and say, "I'm scared and I'm lonely and I'm not sure I can birth a new campaign and a baby."

Amy, Beck's personal assistant and possibly his

lover, jumped into mind. Cady was sure Amy had never felt lonely in her life; with her ebullient and feisty personality she could talk to everybody.

Unfortunately, the person she most wanted to call was Beck.

Back then she'd been able to tell Beck anything and everything. Well, everything besides the truth about her autistic brother. That her parents had sent him to live in a residential home because they hadn't wanted him to live with them anymore. Beck wasn't a fan of her parents, and that knowledge would've amplified that dislike. Neither had she told him that she'd lived her life wondering if her position within their home was equally tenuous.

All her life she'd tried to be perfect and she'd sacrificed relationships in her effort to win the trophy, the election, the prize. Beck had been her first real, intense friendship and she'd loved talking with him, being with him as much as she loved kissing him and making love to him. She'd reveled in his attention and, for the first time since Will was sent away, felt that there was no pressure to be anything other than who she was.

She now realized how little Beck told her about himself. He'd been happy to listen to her ramble on but he'd never opened up to her. She knew his body intimately but nothing of what drove him.

What she thought they'd shared had been very one-sided. And why did that still hurt?

Shaking off her melancholy, she told herself that the power to change was always one decision away.

Tom and her business had been her focus for the last while. Her boyfriend was a married, insensitive asshat, and her business was in intensive care, but she was rid of one and the other was recovering. Once this campaign was finished, when the ground under her feet felt a little more solid, she'd make an effort to be more sociable, to make some new friends.

Or maybe not. People had the habit of turning out to be someone or something you never expected.

Cady heard the rap on her door and frowned. Visitors to her Sunset Park, Brooklyn, apartment needed to be buzzed in. Tom was the only person who'd come to her place in more than a year. Her buzzer hadn't sounded and Cady felt fear lurch up into her throat. Who was at her door so late on a freezing night and what could that person want?

Cady crossed her tiny apartment to the front door and looked through the eyepiece to see the distorted image of Beck on the other side.

Beck? She immediately looked at the clock on her kitchen wall and frowned at the time. Ten-twenty on a Friday night? She expected him to be on a date, eating dinner in a four-star restaurant, in a club or at a party, the things that normal, filthy-rich Manhattan bachelors did on a Friday night.

"I'm growing old here, Collins. Open up."

Through her thin door Cady heard Beck's growly words, so she flipped the three dead bolts open. She yanked the door open, realized that the chain was still on, shut it again, removed the chain and opened the door to Beck.

*Calm the hell down. There's no need to feel so
damn excited at seeing him.*

"You're in Brooklyn? Did you get lost?" Cady
asked, leaning against her door frame so that he
couldn't step into her teeny, tiny apartment. God, his
bathroom was probably bigger than her whole place.

Beck grabbed her elbows, lifted her up and walked
her into her apartment. He placed her on her feet, shut
the door behind him, shot the bolts and shrugged
open his coat.

"Amy said that you need to see me," Beck said,
ignoring her annoyed squawk.

"Yes, during *office* hours."

Beck sat down on her black-and-white-striped
couch and rested his forearms on his thighs. "I'm
here now. Got a beer?"

Cady frowned at his bent head and watched him
as he rubbed his forehead with his fingers as if he
was trying to massage a headache away. He looked
frustrated and exhausted, like the week had kicked
his ass to hell and back.

Cady waved her hand at her small wine rack. "I
have wine. Nothing special, but I can offer you a glass."

Beck stood up and it took him two strides to reach
her galley kitchen and the small wine rack next to
the fridge. He started pulling out bottles to check the
labels and Cady waited for the disparaging comment
at her shoddy taste in wine. Instead he just picked a
bottle of Cabernet and opened it.

He lifted two glasses off the shelf next to the rack,
pouring the ruby liquid into the first glass.

"I don't want any," Cady quickly told him.

Beck lifted an eyebrow. "Why not?"

She couldn't tell him that she was pregnant, so she opted for a quick shrug. "Not in the mood."

After a sip of his wine, he brought his glass and the bottle back to where she was perched on the single chair and resumed his seat.

After a long silence, during which Beck examined her apartment, Cady linked her hands around her knee and spoke. "Why are you here, Beck?"

"Two reasons. The first is that I need to apologize." He stared down into his glass, his mouth tight. "I was wrong to offer you money for you not to take the job. It was insulting and, well…" He looked at her, his eyes troubled. "I didn't like the fact that we got that hot that fast. It was a quick, get-out-of-the-fire-fast reaction."

She understood. She'd felt as disoriented, as shattered as he had obviously. And she couldn't forget that she'd come very close to taking the money and bolting out of there. "Um…okay. Thanks?"

Beck's mouth held the hint of a smile. He sipped his wine and kept his compelling eyes on her face. "The second reason is that Amy told me to give you some time because your begging her for an appointment is driving her nuts."

"Begging is a strong word," Cady replied. "But I do need to talk to you about the campaign."

"Yeah, I know. I'm sorry, I've had a hell of a week." He leaned back and placed an ankle over his knee. "Can we do it now?"

Cady glanced at her desk, tucked into the corner of her tiny apartment, and saw her meticulously organized files, her laptop. She'd brought home everything she needed from her office, but she never liked discussing business in a ratty T-shirt and yoga pants. Still, Beck was here now... She nodded her agreement and then she saw the yawn he tried to hold back, saw the tension in his neck, the exhaustion in his eyes. It was the end of a long week and they were both played out.

"You look tired, Beck."

Beck scrubbed his hand over his face. "It's been busier than usual. Linc has taken a few weeks off. He's dealing with his own personal crisis, so I'm holding down the fort."

As his hands fell, she saw a different Beck from the handsome playboy the world saw online and in the society column. She didn't see the man who was always ready with a smart-alec comment, the well-dressed, ripped, swoon-enticing Bachelor Ballantyne. She saw a man who looked like he'd worked an eighty-hour week. The Ballantyne director with far too much responsibility on his plate. Someone who hadn't had a decent night's sleep or a good meal in far too long.

"Have you eaten?" Cady asked him.

"Lunch, a lifetime ago." Beck took a moment to answer. "I was planning on nuking a frozen pizza when I got home."

Cady wrinkled her nose. She wasn't a great cook, but even she knew that frozen pizzas were nothing more than refined sugars and MSG. "I have some frozen homemade pasta sauce and I can boil some linguine and put out a salad, if you'd prefer real food to fake pizza."

Enthusiasm flickered in Beck's eyes, but it was quickly replaced by regret-tinged determination. "Don't bother. I just came over to see what it was you wanted to discuss with me."

She needed his answers and approvals, but he needed food, decent food. Besides, her brain was so fried she didn't think she could have a clear and detailed conversation about the campaign if he put a ticking time bomb under her butt. And she suspected that Beck wasn't at his best, either.

"It's far too late to discuss business, so we're not going to do that. Pasta and sauce, last chance to say yes."

Beck reluctantly nodded his head.

So, Beck didn't feel comfortable with gestures of kindness and thoughtfulness. Was this something new, or was it something she'd never known about him before? Beck had never really shared himself, so for all she knew he could've come out of the womb walking and talking and trading shares on Wall Street.

And she'd been so caught up with juggling her parents' disappointment in her and her own rebellion, that she never considered he might need to lean on her occasionally.

Shame on her.

In the kitchen, Cady took out the frozen sauce and put it in the microwave to defrost. She placed a pot of water on her small stove and dashed in some salt. "Where is home, by the way?" she asked him after she pulled a ready-made salad from the fridge.

"SoHo."

Of course he lived in the most expensive, trendy area of Manhattan. Where else?

"In a warehouse-converted loft apartment or in a new development?" Cady asked.

"I own the top floor of a warehouse that was converted into apartments in the nineties." Beck slid down so that his head rested on the back of the sofa. "It's a lot of space, but I'm a big guy and I don't like feeling like I'm living in a teacup."

"Then you must feel like this place is a thimble," Cady commented.

Beck looked around. "It is tiny but very you. And those framed mirrors on the wall make it feel a lot bigger than it actually is. And, although I don't think both of us would fit into your kitchen, it has charm."

"Yeah, this is as charming as I can afford."

When it was ready, Cady took the heated sauce from the microwave before moving the pot of pasta to the sink. Using a tiny colander, she drained the pasta, added olive oil, tossed in the sauce and wished she had some Parmesan to grate over the top. When she had a regular income, and time to shop, she promised herself she'd always have cheeses and sauces and herbs in her fridge.

Cady placed a fork and a placemat on the coffee table in front of him, put the plate down and gestured for him to eat. Beck scooted forward and quickly pulled his tie from around his neck. He tossed it in the general direction of his jacket before picking up the fork. "This smells great."

"It tastes better."

Cady curled up into her chair, tucking her feet beneath her bottom and watched Beck eat. He'd always loved food and he'd never hesitated to try something different while they were traveling.

"So good," Beck muttered between mouthfuls.

Cady smiled and rested her head on the back of the chair. Beck was in her apartment, eating her food and looking so hot it made her ache. She wished that she could crawl into his lap, rest her head on his chest and feel his muscled arms around her. He'd always made her feel so protected, like nothing could hurt her. But if she did that, she knew that his big hands would skim her from butt to knee and she'd lift her mouth to nuzzle his throat. He'd sigh, look down at her and she'd drop her head back and two seconds later his mouth would be on hers.

Within another two seconds she'd be naked. And she was not going to get naked with Beckett Ballantyne again! He was her client and she'd learned her lesson with Tom. Naked and business and client were words that shouldn't occur in the same sentence.

Add pregnant to the melee and bad went directly to terrible.

It didn't bear thinking about.

Yawning, Cady tucked a cushion under her head and rested her hand on her still-flat abdomen. Good idea, she told herself. Think about the baby and not

Beck. Come to think of it, she needed to make an appointment with a doctor to have a checkup.

Thinking of the baby made her think of her parents. Her mother had given her a pass on coming home and meeting the church interview committee, but sooner or later she had to inform them that they were going to be grandparents. But she wasn't ready to tell them...she wasn't ready to tell anyone, and especially not Beck. What, exactly would she say? *I've just broken up with my married ex-client and I'm pregnant with his child.*

Married man. Who was also her client. Who made her pregnant. Strike one, two and three. Professional she was not.

But she was determined to be professional with Beck. She'd made enough mistakes confusing business and pleasure, and no matter how sexy Beck was, it would only be business between them. To prove her point, she'd show him how dedicated she was and run through her ideas for the campaign with him at nearly eleven on a Friday night. She'd just wait for Beck to finish his food and then she'd open her eyes and tell him.

Beck looked up and smiled at Cady's open mouth. Her long lashes were smudges on her too-white face. He'd thought she looked tired when he first arrived, but now, her face relaxed in sleep, he could see how exhausted she really was. Her face was thinner as were her arms and thighs, he noticed now as he let his eyes roam down her slight frame.

Cady looked like she needed to go on a month-long diet of hamburgers and milkshakes. Beck placed his fork on his plate and rested his forearms on his knees, happy to take the time to really look at Cady. Thailand Cady had been open and chatty, but this Cady was quieter, stronger, somehow even more attractive. She was mysterious, an enigma, a puzzle he wanted to solve.

And he knew, beyond a shadow of a doubt, that he wanted her under, on top of him, any damn way he could get her.

That hadn't changed.

Beck ran his hand over his jaw and pushed his plate away. How the hell was he going to work with her and be around her without stripping her naked and taking her on the nearest surface or up against the closest wall? And that was the real reason he'd ignored her request for an appointment this week. He'd wanted time to wrap his head around the kiss that they shared, and around the fact that she was back in his life and fifty times as likely to turn it upside down.

He'd needed time to get his need for her under control. To get his life back.

He needed that control.

He'd been in her apartment, in her presence, for less than an hour and he was thinking about picking her up, walking the five steps to her bedroom and, after placing her on the bed, exploring every inch of her skin, kissing her mouth, sliding into her hot, moist channel. He'd dreamed of her for so long and here she was, back in his life.

God, resisting her was torture. Plain and simple. Since time hadn't dulled the attraction between them, he'd been right to push her away all those years ago.

Beck found himself reaching out to push a dark curl off her cheek. He yanked his hand back and shot to his feet, picking up his plate and taking it to the kitchen. He rolled up his sleeves and filled the small sink with hot water, finding the dish soap in a tiny cupboard to his left.

He was bone tired, he thought as he washed her dishes, but after a visit to Cady, sleep wouldn't come easy tonight. It never did. He'd tried meditation and acupuncture and massage, but his brain refused to shut down. Exercising to the point of exhaustion was one of the few ways he could obtain a few hours of sleep.

To this day, making love to Cady was still the only activity that relaxed him enough to fall asleep and stay asleep for any length of time. After she returned to the States, insomnia had quickly become his best friend and he'd assumed sex was the answer. He was an okay-looking guy and sex and backpacking went together like popcorn and beer, so finding someone to share his bed, or tent, or hammock had never been difficult.

When his sleep patterns didn't improve he had to admit that it might've been sex with Cady that relaxed him and not plain sex.

And speaking of sex, he couldn't remember when he'd last had that pleasure, either. Three months ago? Maybe.

He wanted to make love to Cady, and sleep would

be a fantastic side benefit. Beck tossed the dish towel onto the counter and looked across the room to her still-sleeping form. This wasn't all about reliving their past. He also wanted to make love to her because she was still the most fascinating woman he'd ever met. At nineteen, she'd been young and in need of his protection, a role he hadn't minded taking on. But this Cady, fast asleep and breathing deeply, was tougher, stronger and far too compelling for his piece of mind.

She was Cady 2.0, fascinating and so sexy that his breath caught in his throat every time he looked at her. He wanted her.

In his bed.

But not, per se, in his life.

Cady was dangerous, he reminded himself. She had a way of crawling under his skin and digging in. He couldn't allow that, couldn't lose control of this situation. He'd sent her away because she'd become a threat to his self-sufficient, lone-wolf lifestyle, because she made him dream of things he had no right to have. A love of a good woman, happiness, a family, kids. All the stuff he was not entitled to.

He had no intention of allowing Cady Collins to slide under his skin again. He was smarter than that.

And the best way to do that was to keep his distance…especially physically. If he touched her, kissed her, then he'd want to make love to her. So he'd just have to stay at least six feet away from her at all times.

Play it safe, dude.

But damn, he really wanted sex. And sleep.

Five

On Monday, clutching a pile of folders and her tablet to her chest, Cady made her way down the hall to her appointment with Beck. A few feet from Amy's office she stopped when, through the glass walls, she noticed Sage Ballantyne perched on the corner of Amy's desk. The two women were deep in conversation. Not wanting to intrude she turned away, thinking that, since she was ten minutes early, she'd wait at Reception.

"Cady!"

Damn. She couldn't exactly ignore Sage Ballantyne, who was as much her boss as Beck. Cady retraced her steps and stood in the open doorway to Amy's office, feeling uncomfortable.

"I can come back in ten," she stated as she flicked

a look at Beck's office and saw that his glass walls were opaque.

"No, come on in," Sage said on a welcoming smile. "Amy and I were just about to have coffee. My brothers are still in there," she said with a nod to Beck's office. "We've just had a quick partners meeting."

Sage pushed her hands into the back pockets of her faded jeans. She wore a gypsy top and her dark hair was pulled into a messy knot on top of her head. Sage wore no makeup—not that she needed it with such expressive eyes and flawless skin—and she looked nothing like the polished woman who'd politely grilled her at her presentation yesterday.

"That was director Sage, this is artist Sage," Amy said, seeming to read her mind.

"How do you do that?" Cady demanded, placing her tablet and folders on Amy's desk as Sage picked up her desk phone and quickly ordered coffee to be delivered to Amy's office.

"You have a very expressive face." Amy shrugged before pushing her chair back from her desk and crossing her legs. She gestured to the chair on the other side of her desk. "Take a seat. Sage has a million questions."

Oh, God. Cady lifted an eyebrow at Sage. "You do?" she asked, hoping that her cool tone would make her reconsider that decision.

"Honey, I have three older brothers. You need more than an unfriendly look to deflect me," Sage replied with a grin. "So, question one... You are the girl Beck went to Thailand with."

Cady shrugged. "That's not a question, but yes..."

Sage's eyes narrowed. "And you were the one who broke his heart."

Now that was a crazy statement. She wasn't even sure Beck had a heart.

"I went to Thailand with Beck, but Beck sent me home. He broke *my* heart. Besides," she said as she sent Amy a measured look, "I'm presuming he found some willing company as soon as I left."

Amy grinned. "He did. Me."

Yeah, she got it. Beck moved on quickly, proving that he didn't give a fig about her leaving and that his heart hadn't been affected by her departure.

Sage frowned at Amy. "But you said he was miserable for months after she left."

"He was," Amy answered. She flashed a mischievous grin. "But Cady thinks that I comforted him in the tried and tested way."

Sage's eyes widened as laughter crossed her face. "No! Really?"

Cady didn't think any part of this conversation was amusing and she sent a longing look at the door. "Can we talk about something else?"

"She thinks you slept together?" Sage asked Amy, totally ignoring Cady's question. "She doesn't know?"

"Apparently not." Amy's eyes met hers and she smiled. "I'm gay, Cady. Julia is going to be my wife. We've been together for nearly seven years."

What?

Amy exchanged a quick look with Sage and the naughty expression reappeared on her face. "Actually, you caught my eye in Thailand, not Beck."

Again...*what*?

"Stop it, Amy," Sage said. Then she turned to Cady. "Ignore her. She's a chronic flirt. And a world-class troublemaker."

"I am not," Amy protested, placing her hand on her heart in protest. Sage frowned at her and she lowered her hand and shrugged. "Okay, I am. And I was, sort of, joking about eyeing you in Thailand."

Cady stared at her. "But I thought he moved on from me to you."

"Nope. I'm not saying that he didn't move on eventually, but I was his buddy. I still am."

Okay, well... Wow. Cady shook her head, trying to assimilate what she'd just heard. She stared down at her hands, totally confused. If Beck hadn't wanted to move on to a new relationship, then why did he force her to leave?

"Why did you leave Thailand, Cady? You were good together. Anyone could see that." Amy gestured to the intern who entered her office. Once he put down the tray holding a coffee carafe and they were alone again, she looked at Cady. "Well?"

"I didn't leave. He sent me away. He bought me a ticket back home and said it was time for me to go."

"That doesn't make sense," Sage said, frowning.

"Of course it does," Amy scoffed. "It's classic

Beck behavior." Amy looked at Sage. "He pulls back when—"

Amy stopped abruptly and she shared a long look with Sage. Cady caught the flash of warning that arced between them. Cady mentally begged one of them to finish that sentence but Sage busied herself with pouring coffee, and Amy glanced at her computer monitor.

Cady knew that they felt like they'd said too much, that they were being disloyal to Beck by discussing him.

They were and always would be protective of him and she was not, and never would be, part of their inner circle. She was just someone they'd hired and, speaking of, maybe it was time to do that job.

What happened so long ago had absolutely no bearing on her work with Ballantyne International, and she was wrong to discuss the past with Beck's sister, and his employee and friend. It didn't matter that they were being as unprofessional as she was. Sage was a director and Amy a long-trusted employee. It was up to her to apologize. "I'm sorry. That was unprofessional of me, and I shouldn't have brought up the past."

"You didn't. We did," Sage said, flicking a glance over her shoulder. "And we really shouldn't have, either. Beck would skin us alive if he knew."

He would. Beck had no time for office gossip. "Yeah, maybe we can forget this conversation," Cady replied.

"Done," Amy said. "I'm really glad you got the job, Cady. Sage said your presentation was fantastic."

"I'm glad you liked it." Cady took her cup of coffee from Sage and took a sip.

"I love the idea of trying to meld Ballantyne tradition with something new and hip and cool."

Cady looked down at her lap, took a breath and looked Amy in the eye. "Thank you. I am very conscious of how much I owe you."

Amy pulled a face. "No worries. As I said, if Julia hadn't said you were any good, I wouldn't have suggested you pitch. The fact that Beck lights up like a Christmas tree whenever you are around is just an added bonus."

Before she could utter a denial, Beck's voice rumbled out of the intercom on Amy's desk. "Sage, get back to work. Cady, get your ass in here. Amy, is there any point in telling you to do anything?"

Cady's jaw dropped and the cup in her hand wobbled. She sent an anxious look at the still-opaque walls.

Amy grinned as she hit the intercom button to speak. "Nope, you can try, though, boss. You might get lucky."

"Did he hear us?" Cady demanded, not realizing that Sage took her cup from her hand.

Amy shrugged and grinned. "I hope not. I'm going to the ladies' room." She stood up and gestured to the door leading to Beck's office. "Go on in when you're ready."

Cady nodded but stayed in the chair, fighting her urge to bolt.

She couldn't face Beck right now. She needed time to assimilate the fact that Amy wasn't anything more than his friend, that both Sage and she seemed to think that he'd been miserable when she left.

If that was true, then why did he send her away?

Cady shook her head. It didn't matter; none of this mattered. What was important was that she did a sterling, professional job for Ballantyne International, so that she would be able to parlay this one job into more. This was her way to resuscitate her company. And to put cash in the bank.

She was not going to jeopardize that by taking a fruitless stroll down memory lane.

Cady stood up and touched the knot at the back of her hair, conscious that Amy and Sage were staring at her.

"It'll be okay, Cady, I promise." Amy walked out of her office and tossed Cady a sincere smile over her shoulder. "I'm glad you're here. Welcome to Ballantyne International."

Amy closed the door behind her, and Cady turned at Sage's low chuckle. "Sometimes I think that Amy should just change her name to Ballantyne and be done with it."

"And you don't mind that?"

Sage smiled. "Being a Ballantyne is about heart, not name. We became a family when Connor adopted the four of us. We don't get hung up on DNA around here." Sage placed her elegant hand on Cady's forearm and squeezed. "But from me, welcome to our world. I'm glad you're back."

Cady watched Sage walk away and reminded herself that she was just a visitor to their world. Despite her previous relationship with Beck, she wasn't part of their inner circle, and there was no chance that she ever would be.

What she and Beck had was possible in Thailand, a million miles away, where he was just Beck and she was just a girl he'd met at a party. But things were different now. Despite their raging chemistry, the ridiculous physical attraction and the fact that they both didn't want to work together, they had no choice.

He was her client, the man who paid her invoices, her boss.

Nothing remained of the backpackers they once were. This was business.

And that was all it could ever be.

Cady walked over to Beck's door, lifted her hand up to knock and lowered it again. She hadn't seen or spoken to Beck since she'd fallen asleep on him Friday night. It was now Monday and she was still embarrassed that her boss had picked her up from her chair, tucked her into her bed, and washed and dried the dishes she'd used to make him supper before leaving her apartment. And she had just snored on. She knew she snored because he'd left her a note, penned in his strong hand on a bright pink Post-it note from her desk.

You still snore.
Thanks for supper.
—Beck.

Cady didn't think she could be any more embarrassed.

But she had to face Beck right now. And she had to open the door to do it.

Cady knocked and when Beck told her to enter, she did, smiling at Linc and Jaeger. Linc was lounging in Beck's leather chair and Jaeger stood across the room, his shoulder pressed into the wall. She turned to look at Beck and her heart bounced off her rib cage. He stood by the window, the weak sun turning his dark blond hair to gold. A baby boy, who looked to be about a year old, was slapping his hand against Beck's mouth, yanking it away when Beck tried to nibble his fingers. Both of them, man and baby, were laughing.

Cady had to remind herself to breathe. She hadn't seen Beck smile like that, that heart-stopping, heart-breaking smile, since Thailand. It changed his entire face and he looked both ten years younger and ten times sexier.

It was sensory overload, Cady thought. Looking at him was like looking into the sun. If she didn't stop soon, her eyes would melt.

But try as she might, she couldn't pull her eyes away. Watching Beck play with a baby turned her heart to mush. All those years ago, her teenage heart had imagined a scenario like this, Beck playing with his baby, the baby she carried for him. Her life had taken a three-sixty from then. She was back in Beck's life, as his PR person, and she was carrying a baby. But it wasn't his.

It was Tom's… Actually, no. Cady straightened her spine. This baby was hers.

A masculine cough broke the silence and yanked her back into the here and now. She blinked and she was in Beck's office with Linc and Jaeger and a baby who could only be Jaeger's newly discovered son, Ty. Amy had filled her in on the Ballantyne family dynamics and Cady had listened, astonished. Jaeger had recently reunited with Piper, who he'd had a fling with in Milan eighteen months ago. Piper got pregnant then but Jaeger only heard about, and met his son a few months before. Jaeger and Piper, Amy gleefully told her, had wasted no time in expanding their family and Piper was newly pregnant. Linc was a single dad of a four-year-old, having raised Shaw since his mom, Kari, abandoned both of them when Shaw was six weeks old. And, Amy divulged, Kari had done it again and dumped her baby daughter with her sister, Tate, and run off again. Tate was currently living in The Den, working temporarily as Shaw's nanny, but Amy was certain that there was a lot more to that story!

Lives of the rich and famous, Cady thought, intrigued.

"Hand my boy over, Beck," Jaeger said after she'd said a general hello. "We're keeping you and Cady from working."

Beck held Ty like a football and shook his head. "No worries. We're going to discuss the PR campaign and I'd welcome your input."

Linc looked at his watch and shook his head. "Sorry, I have a conference call in five."

Jaeger looked at his own watch and crossed the room to take Ty from Beck. "And Piper just sent me a message that she's downstairs and she's taking Ty home."

Cady smiled as Ty shouted his displeasure at being removed from his uncle's arms. Beck didn't look that happy about it, either. "Are you enjoying living in Park Slope?" Cady asked him, Ty wiggling in his arms.

"Love it." Jaeger flashed his heartthrob smile. "But I'd live in a tent in Prospect Park if that's where Piper and Ty were."

Aw. Sweet guy.

"You are such a sap," Beck muttered, but Cady heard the affection in his voice. He looked at Ty and gently pulled his foot. "Remember our deal, little man. Your first word is going to be Beck."

"Like hell," Jaeger muttered and Cady laughed.

Linc, on his way to the door, bent his knees to look into Ty's face. "Better yet, make it Linc. Anything but Dad, okay?"

"You guys suck," Jaeger muttered as they left the room. Cady heard the door click closed behind them and looked at Beck, who was still standing by the window, sunlight glinting off his hair and his two-day stubble.

"Take a seat," Beck said, walking over to his desk and pulling back his chair so he could sit down. He pushed it away from his desk and placed his ankle on his opposite knee. Cady sat down, crossed her legs, linked her hands around her knee and tried not to squirm under his direct and penetrating gaze. "You still look tired."

Cady felt the heat in her cheeks. "I'm sorry I fell asleep. That was so rude."

"It's not like you fell asleep at the boardroom table, Cady. It was late, and I was in your place, so relax."

"You should've just left me there or shaken me awake. You didn't need to put me to bed." She saw the heat flare in his eyes so she jumped off that subject. "And you definitely didn't need to do the dishes. Though that was probably a novelty for you," she added, teasing him.

Beck's mouth tipped up in a half smile. "For your information, I washed dishes last Sunday night, after our family dinner at The Den."

She knew that was how they referred to their family brownstone. "Have you Ballantynes not heard of a wonderful invention called a dishwasher?"

"Oh, Jo has one, but she doesn't see why we should waste power using it when she has minions to do it for her," Beck stated.

"I always liked her," Cady said, looking at her hands. "Is she still the housekeeper at The Den?"

"No, she retired after Connor died. She stills lives

at The Den and she helps Linc with Shaw, his four-year-old."

"Although I only met them once, I liked both her and Connor."

"He liked you," Beck replied, his voice gruff and growly. Their eyes clashed and memories whirled and swirled between them.

Don't do this, Cady told herself. *Don't get sucked in.*

Whatever it was that existed between her and Beck, it was over and if it wasn't, then it should be. He'd pushed her away once; he'd do it again. Beck was, possibly, more unavailable than he'd been at twenty-three. And there were two of them in the game now. Beck wouldn't want to start anything— even an affair—with a pregnant woman just out of a relationship with her married, ex-client boyfriend.

"We should work." Cady dropped her hot, desperate words into the charged silence between them.

Beck blinked, looked down at his desk, and his shoulders rose and fell. When he lifted his head again, his face was blank and his eyes emotionless. Her old lover was gone and the Ballantyne CFO was back.

Good. She needed the here and now, and didn't need to remember the there and then.

Cady pulled her tablet from her bag and put it on her lap. As she consulted her notes she forced her attention off Beck's wide chest and muscular arms and onto her job. Occasionally she looked out the window but she didn't see the traffic and pedestrians below; she saw magnificent gems, Ballantyne gems, and told him how she intended to reintroduce them to the world.

Cady told Beck about her market research and the results of her brand audit. She touched on the company's weak spots and pointed out areas for innovation and growth. When she finished her report, she tossed out a seemingly random question.

"Of all the pieces of jewelry you've seen pass Ballantyne's, what is your favorite?"

"Wow, change of subject." Beck rubbed his jaw. "I have no idea. I've seen so many valuable stones and exquisite works of jewelry art that it's a hard question to answer."

"What piece of jewelry did you feel most connected to? What makes your heart beat faster?"

"Why are you asking this?"

"Bear with me."

Beck shifted in his chair, looking a little on edge. "Real or imagined? Or lost?"

"Anything. Don't qualify your response. I want your gut reaction."

Beck shifted in his chair and she thought she saw a touch of sadness pass through his eyes. "My mom's engagement ring. It was a magnificent, five carat red beryl stone. Fantastically rare."

Cady saw the pain flash in his eyes and wanted to reach out to him, wanted to offer comfort, but she didn't dare. She maintained her professional demeanor. "Okay, that's your special stone. The Kashmir sapphire Jaeger gave to Piper in her engagement ring is his. Linc, apparently, loves Alexandrite because the stones can be different colors under different light. And Sage has an affinity for red diamonds."

"Because they are so damn rare. And incredibly beautiful," Beck said. "Where are you going with this, Cady?"

"I want to do a series of print ads around each Ballantyne and the gems you love. I would suggest we start with Jaeger and Piper, and ride the wave of interest around their engagement. I want to get those ads out in time for Valentine's Day."

"That's less than a month away."

She was aware of that. She was also aware that pulling this off would require long days and longer nights. "In addition to Piper's ring, Linc has, according to Amy, a magnificent Alexandrite ring he inherited from Connor Ballantyne, and then there's the one I can't wait to see—a red diamond, platinum and diamond flower ring that's in your uncle's private collection that Sage loves."

Cady tapped her finger against her tablet and brought up the mock-up she'd put together. "I'd feature each of you in an ad—relaxed and accessible, white shirt, blue jeans, bare feet—and holding your priceless jewelry. The public will have to go online to read up on why that piece in particular speaks to you. We'll advertise Sage's new, modern designs on those pages, as well. And when the ads launch, I want to do a function to exhibit those jewels and others in the Ballantyne collection."

"That's not possible," Beck said through gritted teeth.

"Why not?" Cady demanded.

"First, those gems are worth a freaking king's ransom and they'd need extraordinary security measures if they're going to be shown to the public."

"Not the public. Only rich, hip, hot, young celebs will see the exhibition," Cady told him, enjoying herself. "And I've already contacted a company specializing in jewelry exhibitions. They haven't lost a gem yet. Speaking of, where's your mom's ring?"

Beck didn't crack a smile. "Somewhere on that mountain where they crashed."

She heard the pain in his voice and again Cady wanted to wrap her arms around him. Such pain. There was nothing to say so she sent him a sympathetic smile. But that meant she'd have to find another piece of jewelry to connect to Beck. "I'm sorry, Beck. Is there another piece we can use that you feel strongly about?"

Beck linked his hands around the back of his head. "I like the idea, the connection between old and new. Could we use a paste copy of my mom's ring?"

"You have one of those?"

"Every time an important piece comes through here, a copy—and an excellent imitation—is made for our records."

"We'd have to explain that it's the copy, but it'll work. Great." Energized by his reception of her ideas, Cady stood up. Her mind was reeling with plans as she walked to the window, resting her palm on the thick glass as she envisioned the exhibit. Then she sent him an uncertain look. "It might dredge up some memories for you and your siblings."

"The memories are always there, so there's nothing to dredge up," Beck said as he walked toward her. When he stood in front of her, he ran his hand over her hip and skimmed his knuckles across her abdomen. "Animation and excitement suits you, Cades."

Cady saw the heat in his eyes and she shook her head. "Don't do this, Beck."

"I want you."

"It's not a good idea," Cady told him, sucking in a deep breath as his knuckles skimmed the underside of her suddenly sensitive breasts.

Beck placed his palms on the glass, bracketing her head. He looked down at her, desire on his face and, Cady ascertained with a quick glance down, in his pants.

"Beck...please."

"What are you asking me to do, Cady? Kiss you? Touch you? Let you go? You're going to have to be more specific."

Damn, what did she want? Him, same as always. She shouldn't, Cady thought, but she lifted her hand and brushed her fingers against his rough jaw. She didn't want to say the words. If she did, she couldn't take them back, couldn't rewind. Couldn't blame him for taking the decision out of her hands.

He was leaving the decision to kiss him up to her. If she asked him to let her go, he would. Conversely, if she asked him to kiss her, touch her, taste her, he'd rock her world. So much time had passed, so much had happened, but she was still inexplicably drawn to him. Cady knew it was smarter to walk away, but how could she ignore the flash of masculine appreciation in his eyes, the catch in his breath when they touched? When it came to Beck she'd never been smart and nothing, it seemed, had changed.

They'd always had the ability to spark off each other and she knew that if he kissed her, they'd both go up in flames. They were that volatile.

God, she wanted to burn under his touch.

"Ask me to kiss you, Cady." Beck clasped her face in his hands, his thumbs rubbing the arch of her cheekbones.

Cady meant to push him away, but instead her hands ran from his wrists to his biceps, enjoying the power in his muscles. "Kiss me, Beck. Properly, intensely, like you mean it."

His eyes flashed and when she touched her bottom lip with the tip of her tongue, he swooped down. Beck slanted his lips over hers, and time and space and thought rolled away as she lost herself in his arms. Or had she found herself?

Her fingers curled into his hair and she pushed her breasts against his chest. Beck was more powerful now than he'd been at twenty-three. Cady could feel it in the arms wound around her butt and back, in the hands pulling her into him. His mouth was sweeter and hotter than she remembered, his body bigger and harder, and her response more fervent and insistent. How was she going to step away, to get back to business when her heart and mind and body demanded more?

Beck groaned, jerked his mouth off hers and rested his forehead on the top of her head. "I wasn't going to do this. I really wasn't."

Cady pushed her hands against his chest to put some distance between them and when his hands fell from her body, she took another step back. "Me neither. We can't go back, Beck. Not to that."

Beck shoved a hand into his hair and looked irritated. "You talk as if we have a choice."

"We're adults, Beck. We always have a choice." All her mistakes up to this point had been because she'd made some stupid choices and she couldn't take any more chances. She felt like a cat on number eight of her nine lives.

"I cannot, I will not, jeopardize this job and my relationship with Ballantyne International because we have something bubbling between us."

"Those are two totally separate issues."

She'd lost Tom's business because she'd slept with him, because she was stupid enough to think that she could mix business and pleasure.

"That's what you men always say until pleasure and business collide and someone—usually the woman and the one needing the business—gets screwed." Cady winced at the bitterness in her tone.

Beck gripped her chin and forced her to look up into his hard, unyielding face. "Don't judge me by someone else's yardstick, Cady. I'm my own man and if I say that what happens between us physically won't impact on business, then you can believe it."

Yeah, she didn't think so. She'd learned that lesson and learned it well. "It's better not to start anything that might blow up in our faces." Cady pushed her hair off her forehead and placed her hands on her hips. "I need to get back to work. I also need to convince Jaeger and Linc that these ads will work. They really don't want to get in front of a camera."

"I'm not fond of the idea myself," Beck replied. "But I can see why it will work. It's a good concept. Come to dinner at The Den on Sunday night and we can all discuss it then."

Dinner at The Den, the family brownstone, was a Ballantyne tradition. She remembered him telling her that it was a time for the family to reconnect, to wind down, to talk. Her presence there would be an intrusion; Beck could talk his brothers into doing the shoot, he didn't need her.

Besides, being around the Ballantynes as a group reminded her of the family she'd always wanted but knew she'd never have. The kind of family she wanted for her baby.

"I don't think so."

Beck sent her a long look and Cady struggled to keep her face blank. When he turned those piercing, smart and questioning eyes on her, she wanted to hurl her deepest fears and most secret desires at his feet. *Not a good idea*, Cady told herself.

She knew from past experience that she was the only one who could, and should, shoulder her baggage.

Cady injected starch into her spine and picked up her mind map. "You said that there are paste copies of all the important pieces. Can I look at them, including the one of your mom's engagement ring?"

Beck gave her a sharp nod. "Ask Amy to get them for you on the way out. The copy of the red beryl ring is in my safe at home." He glanced at his watch. "I have a business lunch at Sam's but I can stop at my apartment before I go to lunch. I'll be done by two-thirty. If you can meet me at Sam's then I can give it to you."

Sam's was only the finest restaurant in New York City. A haunt for the rich and famous, where a booking had to be made six to eight months in advance. And this was where Beck conducted business lunches? She was so out of his league.

"Sam's at two-thirty. I'll see you there."

Six

After a punishing routine followed by a half hour swim in the private gym in the basement of his apartment building, Beck let himself into his apartment and toed off his trainers at the front door. Dumping his gym bag next to the hall table, he walked across the expansive loft to his gourmet kitchen and grabbed a bottle of water. After gulping it down, he looked out the tinted windows at the incredible view of the city skyline.

He had another crazy day ahead of him trying to keep on top of both his and Linc's work. Linc, thanks to the arrival of Tate and baby Ellie—Kari, Linc's ex, had dumped her baby girl on Tate and done another runner—was running himself ragged, so Beck was picking up the slack. In between running a billion-dollar corporation with offices all over the world, he was also trying to make sense of Cady's dropping back into his life.

He was still insanely attracted to her. And he didn't like feeling this off balance, like he was trying to navigate the rapids of a treacherous river in a leaky bucket. He wasn't used to feeling so out of control, so unsure. The women he dated—okay, slept with—were smart, gorgeous and, well, forgettable. There was only one woman he'd never been able to forget. Who, like a burrowing bug, had crawled into his brain and stayed there.

And she was back.

Cady.

Back then and now, Cady made him want something more than the life he had. Oh, his life was good, he knew that—he was strong, smart, wealthy and successful—but Cady made him want more. Friendship, companionship, having someone to come home to at the end of the day. Someone to fill this empty space with laughter, conversation, music. Someone who made him want to slow down, to chill.

Sex on tap would be great, too.

But a relationship like that wasn't in the cards for him. His parents had a fantastic marriage; they'd been crazy in love with each other, like Jaeger and Piper. Beck hoped that Sage and Linc found the person they could be that happy with. But he didn't deserve that sort of happiness himself.

Intellectually, he knew that he was being hard on himself and that his request for his parents' type of love was normal, even expected. But his neediness had such massive consequences and that was what he couldn't wrap his head around. That was where he stalled. If he started to need someone again, what would the consequences be? If he fell in love and that person was hurt or, God forbid, killed, he wouldn't be able to live with himself. He'd survived his parents' deaths by keeping busy, and he'd earned his place in his family by being smart, hardworking and responsible.

Falling in love, exposing his heart, was irresponsible. And it was simply not happening. So he needed to stay away from Cady. He needed to keep a physical and, most important, an emotional distance from her.

Beck drained the last of the water and tapped the rim against a pane of wet glass. Maybe he'd escape New York, Cady and this cold weather by visiting the Hong Kong and Tokyo branches of Ballantyne's. Both managers had issues that he needed to resolve.

He could take a week, get his head on straight, and maybe even do a surprise visit to the Dubai store on his way back. Or the LA store if they flew in the other direction. Either way, it would put thousands of miles between him and Cady.

Beck heard the chime that informed him that someone was leaning on his buzzer and he frowned. His brothers and sisters had the code to open the front door but none of them would be at his door at six forty-five in the morning. Jaeger would be snuggled up to Piper, Sage needed a bomb to get her out of bed in the mornings and Linc was out of town.

Beckett walked to his front door and pushed the intercom button. "Yeah?"

"Beck, it's me, Cady. We have a problem."

Judging by Cady's stressed-out tone, he knew it was a big one. Beck released the lock on the front door and told her to come on up.

Cady at the crack of dawn. Yeah, this had to be a big-ass problem.

When Cady stepped out of the elevator and saw Beck standing in his doorway she had one thought. Someone dressed in an old, sweat-stained T-shirt, athletic shorts and worn trainers had no right to look like he stepped off the cover of a men's health and exercise magazine. The old jeans and college sweatshirt she wore under her thigh-length coat didn't look half as good on her as ratty clothes looked on him. She wore no makeup, had pulled her hair up into a lopsided ponytail and had just remembered to brush her teeth.

That was what happened when you found out, online, that you were engaged to one of the most eligible bachelors in the city.

Beck stepped back and gestured for her to come into his apartment, so Cady did. He hung her coat up on a metal coat stand that looked like it cost more than the small car she wanted but couldn't afford. Cady jammed her hands into the pockets of her sweatshirt and looked around his loft conversion. She liked the large windows and the exposed red brick walls. The laminated floors were stylish and contemporary as were the oversize, minimalistic, L-shaped, oatmeal-colored couch and the armless leather chairs. The large ornamental lemon tree in the corner needed water.

It was stylish and it was rich, but it didn't have much soul, Cady decided. Apart from a large photograph of Connor and the four Ballantyne siblings, there was little in this apartment that told Cady who lived here. A large wooden door led to what she thought might be a second bedroom, and a steel, spiral staircase led to the suspended master bedroom.

Yeah, rich. Contemporary. She preferred her colorful rabbit hutch in Brooklyn.

Beck stepped into the kitchen area and took a mug from a cupboard above his coffee machine and held it up. "Coffee?"

Eeew, no. Morning sickness had her stomach churning and she was a hairsbreadth away from tossing her cookies. Coffee would send her right over the edge.

"I don't suppose you have any tea? Something with ginger in it?" Cady asked, knowing that her chances weren't good.

Beck opened a narrow cupboard and she saw a large range of herbal teas. "You drink tea?" she asked, incredulous, as he pulled a tea bag from a yellow box.

"I spent enough time in the Far East, I should," Beck said, turning on the luxury coffee machine to make hot water.

It was the first time he'd mentioned traveling and she wondered if he'd ever thought of the time they'd spent together. He probably remembered being frustrated because she was always checking her phone, always crying after speaking to her parents.

Maturity and hindsight made her admit that she hadn't been the best traveling partner, and Beck had been incredibly patient.

From this vantage point Cady could see more decoration on the wall to the left of the front door. A series of enlarged black-and-white photographs. Immediately she recognized the stunningly beautiful bay, encircled by huge cliffs. Looking at the photographs, she could almost feel the silky soft white sand and feel the tropical warmth of the exceptionally clear water.

"I remember you taking these pictures. You got up at some ridiculous hour so that the beach would be empty of people," Cady commented, pleased to hear that her voice was steady. "Later that morning I decided to keep traveling with you and the next day I was on a plane home, my life turned upside down."

Beck gripped the edges of the counter and looked at her, his face expressionless. "That was always the plan, Cady. I never asked you to stay."

"You're right. You didn't and I assumed too much." Cady shrugged. "My bad."

She perched on a very uncomfortable, stainless-steel bar stool on the dining room side of the sleek counter.

"We were young, Cady, and crazy attracted to each other. It couldn't last," Beck said slowly, his voice emotionless.

Lust didn't explain why her world stopped turning, why she'd cried for three months straight and felt hollow for another six. It was fear of trusting and being hurt again that had her avoiding men and relationships for years, dating occasionally but never inviting a man back into her bed and her life. Tom had been the only one she'd taken a risk on, and that decision just reinforced her belief that her choice in men wasn't to be trusted.

Beck filled her cup with hot water and pushed it toward her. He leaned against the counter. "I'm sorry if I hurt you, Cady."

"You did hurt me."

Beck stepped forward and touched her hand with the tips of his fingers. "I really am sorry but I wasn't ready for a relationship with you then."

Then? What did that mean? Was he ready for one now?

Beck shook his head in answer to the question he must've read in her eyes. "I'm not relationship material, Cady. I don't do relationships and I don't do long-term."

Cady made herself ask the question. "What do you do?"

"Sex." Beck's answer was as blunt as her question.

After Tom's lies, his honesty was refreshing. "Fair enough."

"And you, what are you looking for?" Beck asked, his lips thin and his eyes wary.

Cady stared down at the hot tea, inhaling the ginger aroma and praying it would settle her stomach. Once upon a time she wanted to be married, have a family, be happy. Her teenage dreams were all so airy fairy, so intangible. She was older now and a lot more practical. She wanted to reemploy the handful of staff she'd had to let go, renew her office lease, put some money in the bank and stop feeling like she was constantly fighting nausea and losing.

Having a relationship, falling for someone— Beck—was out of the question. Apart from the fact that she'd just ended one relationship, she couldn't forget that Beck had emotionally slaughtered her heart and then tossed the pieces into what felt like a cold, dark, continuous blizzard. Cady felt a shiver run through her and remembered what it felt like to have ice in her veins.

Not again. Never again.

"I'm not looking for anything, Beck. From you or from anyone else," Cady stated, her eyes meeting his. One heartbreak a lifetime was more than enough.

Beck nodded once, abruptly, but his shoulders dropped a notch and she thought she saw him exhale a relieved sigh. Cady wanted to roll her eyes but resisted.

It's okay, Beck. I'm not here to complicate your life.

Oh, wait, she was.

"Congratulations," she said without any preamble, "we are, apparently, engaged."

Cady smiled at the panic that hit his eyes. "I haven't had any caffeine yet, so I'm a bit slow. Would you like to explain that?"

She supposed she should. Beck pushed a button on the state-of-the-art machine and Cady heard the sound of beans grinding and then the distinctive smell of coffee wafted over to her. Once again, her stomach twisted and her throat closed. *Oh, God, morning sickness, go away!*

Cady took a sip of her hot tea and breathed through her mouth. "I woke early and I couldn't sleep, so I thought I'd get a jump on my day. When I started working on this campaign, I set up numerous internet alerts on Ballantyne's, because I wanted to know what was being said about the company. I had fifty messages in my inbox this morning, directing me to websites with breaking news."

Cady rested her elbows on the granite counter and placed her chin in the palm of her hand. "Sam's is a favorite hangout for the paparazzi to find photos of celebs. Yesterday one of those bottom feeders caught the exact moment when you handed over the copy of your mom's ring and I—"

Beckett put down his coffee cup and groaned. "You put the ring on the ring finger of your left hand and held your hand up to look at it. And the photographer assumed he saw an engagement."

Well, nobody could ever accuse Beckett of being slow on the uptake.

"Essentially," she said. "A little research added the details to that scenario. Your mom's ring was well documented and it was immediately assumed that you were giving her ring to me."

Beck gripped the edge of the counter and let loose with a curse.

"Adding depth to the story, they know exactly who I am and that we spent two months traveling together years ago," Cady told him.

Beck's head jerked up. "How the hell would they know that?"

"We were kids. We used the social media sites, and those photos of us together are probably still out there," Cady said, trying to keep calm. One of them had to.

"We need to decide how we're going to manage this," she added, switching into PR mode.

"What do you suggest?" Beck asked. "Are we going to deny it, run with it, ignore it?"

He was a smart guy and Cady wanted to know how he would manage this crisis. "What would you do?"

Beck sipped his coffee and took some time to answer her. "I'm usually pretty decisive but I'm actually not sure. If we deny that we're seeing each other, then we'd have to explain why we were meeting at Sam's, why I was showing a PR person my mom's ring. That would raise questions about why Ballantyne's needs PR. The press might start speculating about whether the brand is as strong as it once was. That, in turn, might have an impact on the price of Ballantyne shares. That's something we don't need, especially since we have concerns about someone who's snapping up large blocks of Ballantyne shares."

Beck's expression indicated that he wasn't going to discuss that any further, so Cady returned to the original problem.

"An astute journalist might ask those questions. I'd prefer to keep the rebranding a secret until the last possible moment. The campaign has more impact that way," Cady said.

Beck pinned her to her seat with a hard look. "Are you suggesting that we stay engaged and keep the rebranding a secret?"

Oh, hell... Cady closed her eyes and hauled in a long, deep breath. "It's not that simple."

"Oh, God, what now?" Beck demanded. He held up his hands, gesturing her not to answer. "Wait, I need more coffee to continue this conversation."

Cady was happy to delay the inevitable, to take a moment to gather her courage. She had to tell Beck that she was pregnant, that if they pretended to be engaged, the world would assume that he was the father of her child. Pretending to be engaged was one thing but his assuming responsibility for her pregnancy was another.

Beck placed his refilled cup of coffee next to her tea, and the smell of coffee traveled up her nose and hit the back of her throat. Cady felt her stomach lurch. She slapped her hand across her mouth and swallowed it back. She wasn't going to be sick. She wasn't.

Cady felt a strong hand on her back and opened her eyes to see Beck holding a small trash bin below her. She grabbed the stainless-steel bin with both hands, ducked her head and threw up.

Cady sat up and took the napkin Beck held out to her and wiped her mouth. Mortified, she hugged the bin to her side and looked at him through teary eyes.

"So, there's a reaction to getting engaged I hadn't expected," Beck said. "Trust me, Cades. It would be a fake engagement. I'm the last person in the world who intends to marry."

"I know that!" Cady told him. "There's just one complication..."

"What?"

"I'm pregnant. And you, obviously, are not the father."

"Oh, crap."

Beck stared at himself in the bathroom mirror, his eyes bleak and his face a shade paler than normal. His hands gripped the edges of the vanity as he tried to assimilate the news he'd just heard.

Cady. Pregnant. Which, the last time he'd heard, meant that she was going to have a freakin' baby.

Dear God in heaven.

Beck lifted his hand up and saw that it was trembling. He shook his head and had to wonder why he was feeling so gob-smacked and sideswiped. He hadn't seen her for nearly a decade and they'd shared a couple of hot kisses so he wasn't entitled to feel pissed off, disappointed or judgmental.

He had a relationship with her almost ten years ago and, whether he was attracted to her or not, he had no right to feel… Exactly how did he feel? Jealous. The thought of someone else loving her, touching her, tasting her fabulous skin, kissing her luscious mouth, made the content of his stomach bubble and boil.

Jealously was not an emotion he was familiar with.

They'd been apart for almost a decade and he'd had other women, lots of women, so he had to accept that she would've had other men in her life. He could accept it…but he didn't have to like it.

Stop emoting and start thinking, Ballantyne!

Forcing his emotions aside, Beck started to think. Before he excused himself to take a shower, she'd briefly explained that she'd been in a relationship, that her ex had no interest in being a father and she no longer wanted to be with him. Getting pregnant hadn't been her intention. It just happened.

Beck picked up his toothbrush to brush his teeth for the second time that morning, needing any excuse to stay in the bathroom for a little longer. Cady's face, her big eyes and her sexy mouth popped up in his brain, and his junk stirred to life. Huh. So the news that she was carrying someone else's kid didn't affect his attraction to her. He still wanted her in the worst way possible.

Beck rinsed, spat and admitted that if this was any other woman handing him the same news, there would be skid marks from him running out of her life at a hundred miles an hour. He would not, for one second, be able to be with, sleep with or date a pregnant woman. It was a perfect recipe for disaster—too many hormones and emotions and physical changes. It was also natural for a woman to look for a mate when she was pregnant, to look for someone to hold her hand, to feel a little less alone. To have someone to nest with.

He wasn't a nesting type of guy.

But this was *Cady*, who was unlike every other woman he'd ever met.

When he pushed away his jealousy at the thought of some cretin making love to her, he realized that her being pregnant didn't fundamentally change his opinion of her. He didn't want to bolt out of her life and, yeah, he still wanted to sleep with her.

He tested his forehead to check if he didn't have a fever.

Beck left his bathroom and walked into his closet, pulling out the first hanger he laid his hand on. Dropping his towel, he quickly dressed and ran his hands and then a brush through his wet hair. How should he handle her surprise announcement?

With the truth, he thought, as he knotted his tie. Nothing, really, had changed. He still didn't want a relationship with her, or anyone else, but her being pregnant didn't change his desire for her.

Sure, sleeping together was complicated. She was just out of a relationship, she was pregnant, he was her client, after all. But she was still a woman and he was still a man and they were still attracted to each other.

Desire didn't stop to read the warning labels.

He'd play this by ear, Beck decided, stepping out of his bedroom. He'd take it day by day, week by

week, if he had to. But he was adult enough and experienced enough to know that pregnant or not, Cady
would, at some point, be in his bed again.

Seven

While Beck took a shower, Cady sat on his couch, clutching the cup of ginger tea. Thankful for some time alone, she thought back to his expression when she'd made her announcement. To say he looked shocked was an understatement, but she couldn't blame him for the string of curses he'd let fly.

He was a guy who wasn't into commitment or relationships, only quick flings, and she was damn sure that having a quick fling with a pregnant woman was not on his bucket list. Even if they did share a history and were madly attracted to each other.

Beck was too into control to be caught up in such an unstable, potentially highly dramatic situation. As for her, she was borderline nuts to be even thinking about Beck in this way. She had enough emotional, physical and financial problems without adding the complication of sleeping with that delicious slab of muscle.

Man, her life was so messed up. For someone who'd always tried so hard to do the right thing, who pursued perfection, she was surrounded by chaos.

Cady stared at her fingers and wished that Beck would come down from his room. Sitting here, wondering what he was thinking, hoping that he wasn't judging her too harshly, had her palms sweating. Cady knew that she shouldn't care what he thought of her. She was an adult and she should be over wanting anyone's approval. But Beck wasn't just anyone. He was an important part of her life.

She still respected him and he was her client. And, dammit, when she pushed her lust away, she still liked him. He was, and always had been, a good man.

Cady heard his footsteps and watched Beck walk down the spiral stairs, freshly shaved and his hair damp from his shower. She watched as he shoved his arms into a navy blazer, perfectly complementing his white dress shirt worn under a thin berry-colored sweater. Slim-fit wool pants in dark gray covered his long legs, and his trendy sneakers added a hip touch to his outfit. Between Thailand and now, T-shirt-and-cargo-shorts-wearing Beck had morphed into a clotheshorse, Cady thought. She looked down at her baggy sweatshirt and thought that she really had to up her game.

Beck walked over to her and sat on the backless leather chair facing her. "So, pregnant, huh?"

Cady couldn't see any judgment in his eyes or distaste on his face.

She nodded glumly. "Yep."

"Are you okay? Any problems?"

"Apart from the puking and the tiredness that I understand is normal, no." Cady gripped her teacup with both hands. Thinking that he might think she was whining, Cady straightened her back. "I'm perfectly able to manage this campaign, Beck."

"I never doubted that for a second," Beck replied, his voice steady. "I just need to know that you're healthy."

Cady nodded, touched by his concern. "I'm fine. I haven't seen a doctor yet but I will."

Beck nodded and stood up. He walked over to the window and leaned into the red brick wall. "And the father? Is he out of the picture?"

"Very. I was going to break up with him before I found out about the baby, but his insistence that I have an abortion nailed that coffin closed."

"Is he an utter moron? You're a pastor's kid."

Cady smiled at his understanding. "My decision to keep my baby goes deeper than that." Should she tell him about Will? Would he understand? "Do you remember that I had a brother?"

A small frown appeared above Beck's nose. "Yeah, he died when you were fifteen, right? From something... Sorry, I can't remember that part."

"I'm touched that you remember that much. Yeah, he had Lupus and he got pneumonia. The virus attacked his lungs and he passed away."

"I'm sorry, Cady."

Her smile just touched the corners of her mouth. "What I never told you is that he was autistic and disabled. I adored him, and he was my best friend, despite his limitations. When I was ten, I came home from school and my grandmother was there instead of Will and my mom. She told me that they'd taken Will to live in a residential home and that it was best for Will that there weren't any long, drawn-out good-byes. He was, as my grandmother put it, becoming 'difficult to handle.'"

"What did she mean by that?"

"I have no idea. The Will I knew was funny and kind and…good."

Beck looked empathetic and interested, unlike Tom who'd just yawned his way through her story. "I was devastated. I've never understood why my parents shipped him off, but that's another story." Cady placed her hand on her stomach. "This child didn't do anything wrong and he or she shouldn't be disposed of because it's more convenient for me."

"Is that what you believe your parents did? Made life more convenient for themselves by sending your brother away?"

Cady stared at him, his words rolling around her head and then crystallizing. That was exactly what she thought and never been able to verbalize. Unwelcome tears burned her eyes. Trust Beck to put his finger on the essence of the problem.

And that was why his words at the airport in Thailand scoured her soul. Sending her away had been so convenient for him.

Beck sat down next to her and, with the pad of his thumb, wiped a tear from under her eye. "Then good for you, for keeping this baby, for taking the harder, less convenient path."

Cady gripped his wrist, holding on to his strength, his warmth. "I'm scared, Beck."

"Raising a kid is a scary thing. But you should also remember that you are bright and capable and so much stronger than you think you are." Beck tipped her chin up. "You can do this, Cades. I promise."

Cady let out a small laugh and felt his strength flow into her. She could do this. After all, it wasn't like she had a lot of choice.

"Thanks," she said, leaving her hand on his wrist. It felt good to touch him again.

"Have you told your parents about the baby?" Beck asked.

Cady sent him an "are you friggin' insane?" look that he quickly and correctly interpreted. His mouth twitched with amusement. "Let me rephrase that... Are you going to tell them?"

Cady shrugged and sighed. "They're going to hit the roof. Dad is also up for a promotion, so hearing that I'm pregnant and single will not be well received." Cady shook her head and made a quick decision. "I don't think I will, not yet. After all, this baby isn't going anywhere."

"Or you can tell them that we're engaged and that

you're pregnant. They'll assume it's mine and we don't have to correct them."

"You'd do that for me?"

"Listen, I am one of the few people who know how over the top your parents can be. What's worse, being engaged and pregnant or single and pregnant?"

When he put it like that, Cady was tempted to agree. But using Beck as an excuse would be like taking the twenty thousand dollars he offered her to walk away from Ballantyne International. It would be taking the easy route. If she was old enough to have sex and get pregnant then she was old enough to be truthful about it.

"Delaying telling my parents is one thing but I can't flat out lie to them."

Beck nodded. "Fair enough."

"Speaking of lying…" Cady wrinkled her nose. "What are we going to do about the engagement?"

"Nothing," Beck stated, his tone suggesting that she not argue.

"What? Why?"

"If we deny it, we look like we have something to hide. If we confirm it, we step into the scamming-the-public-for-publicity territory and that makes me feel uncomfortable. So we do neither and let people think what they want. They will anyway."

It went against every instinct she had as a public relations expert. Situations like these had to be managed, steered, directed. "I don't know if I agree with you, Beck. It could blow up in our faces."

"Whatever scenario we choose could blow up. By

not commentating, confirming or denying, we give ourselves room to move."

Cady could see that he'd made up his mind and that there was no point in arguing. "Okay, well, then I suggest that you call your family and give them a heads-up."

"Don't need to. If I was engaged for real, they'd know about it before the news hit the public space. Would your parents hear about this?"

Cady shook her head. "I very much doubt it. They live an insular life." She glanced at her watch and seeing the time, told herself she needed to get going. She had a long day ahead of her, and Beck, she was sure, was anxious to get to work. "Okay, we'll play it by ear. I should go."

Beck placed his hand on her knee to keep her seated. "It's been a pretty intense morning but there's one more issue we need to address."

There was?

"Okay. What?"

"The fact that every time we're together we're only a heartbeat away from stripping each other naked and doing what we always did best."

Cady looked at him, her mouth half open. What the hell was he talking about? "Beckett, I'm pregnant."

"I heard. I understood."

"I'm pregnant, so you can't want me anymore," Cady stated, comprehensively confused.

Beck rubbed his hand over his jaw and she saw frustration and annoyance flash in his eyes. "I wish

I was that shallow. It would be a lot more convenient. But… I still want you, and I probably always will."

Cady placed her palms together and rested the edges of her fingers on her mouth. He was being open and honest and she should be, too.

"I feel like it's wrong to be this attracted to you, that I should have absolutely no interest in the opposite sex, that all my mental focus should be on my baby," Cady said, confused.

"But it's not?" Beck demanded.

She shook her head.

He rubbed the back of his neck. "I think that's a societal expectation, that you should put your life on hold for this child. But the fact is that you are a sexy woman and we've always had a combustible chemistry. That doesn't go away just because you're pregnant."

Before she could respond, Beck continued. "Don't look so worried, Cady. I'm not about to jump you." He smiled. "Not that I don't want to…and that's what I'm trying, with very little finesse, to say. Whatever this craziness is between us, you're in control of it. I want you but I also understand that your life is crazy at the moment. I know you're stressed and that you have enough to deal with without me trying to coerce you into bed."

Cady looked at him, trying to make sense of his words. Beck was putting her needs above his, and her heart thumped at his sensitivity. And his generosity.

"And when you decide that the time is right for

us to make love, just say the word," he added with a small smile.

Cady tipped her head to the side, smiling. "Which particular word is that, Beck?" she teased.

He touched her lower lip with his thumb. "It won't matter what you say. I'll see it in your eyes, Cades. I always could and that hasn't changed."

The air between them felt charged with electricity, and Cady knew that it would be so easy to step into his arms, to allow him to make toe-curling love to her. But it wasn't a good idea, and sleeping with him might be another mistake. It had been an emotional, roller-coaster morning and it was smarter, safer, if she stepped back and thought before she acted.

She wanted Beck but damn, there was a high probability that he would be just another in a long line of blunders.

Beck must've seen her decision in her eyes because he lowered his thumb and he stepped away. Cady felt disappointed and immediately second-guessed her decision.

She didn't want to be an adult anymore. It wasn't half as much fun as they'd told her it would be.

When Cady made the arrangements for Jaeger's photo shoot at his home in Park Slope, Brooklyn, she'd expected it would be just her, Jaeger, the stylist and makeup artist, the photographer and his assistant, and maybe Piper and Ty.

She hadn't expected his siblings to head for Brooklyn after work. Linc and his son, Shaw, arrived first and then Sage arrived and with her, Amy. Thank God they were nearing the end of the shoot because Piper's apartment was now full to overflowing. Linc found Jaeger's liquor stash and was handing out drinks while she and the photographer tried to placate the increasingly impatient Jaeger.

When Ty escaped from Sage and bolted across the floor into the picture frame, Jose, the photographer, threw up his hands and eagerly reached for the bottle of red wine Linc left on the mantel. And that, Cady quickly realized, was the end of the shoot.

Her feet ached, her head was on fire and all she wanted to do was go home and have a long, long soak. She was exhausted.

"Cady, these are amazing!"

Cady looked at Sage, who was standing next to Jose looking at the screen of his camera. Judging by Sage's enthusiasm, the shoot wasn't a complete bust. Maybe there was a photo or two they could use for the campaign.

Cady walked out of the study and into Piper and Jaeger's living area and dropped into the corner of the sofa. She really enjoyed the Ballantyne bunch but, God, they were loud! Shaw was chasing a just-walking Ty around the apartment, weaving their way in between adult legs and laughing like loons. Linc was teasing Jaeger about one thing or another and the others were discussing a photography exhibition they'd apparently all seen.

She'd been raised in a quiet, ordered, disciplined house, and the noise and laughter felt like a red hot poker was being repeatedly jammed in her ear. She just wanted to cry. Pregnancy hormones, she told herself. Perfectly normal.

It was and it wasn't, Cady admitted, resting her forearm over her eyes. Yeah, she was a hormonal stew but there was more to this melancholia than a little noise and exhaustion. Working with Beck and fighting her attraction to him was taking its toll. They'd spent a lot of time together lately, both at work and at his apartment—using work as an excuse. They always did *some* work, but they spent more time talking, reconnecting.

And she remembered how much she liked him, how much she simply loved being with him. Since that morning he'd told her that she would have to make the next move, he hadn't once tried to kiss her but she knew he wanted to.

And, God, how she wanted him. She wanted to feel his muscles bunch and move under his hot skin, taste the slight tang of his manly skin. She wanted to nibble the long cord in his strong neck, run her hands through the light layer of hair on his chest. She wanted to feel his hands on her body, his weight on her as he settled over and into her, listen to him gasp in pleasure, sigh in sleep.

She wanted him. She needed him. She couldn't have him.

Because she couldn't afford to forget that he'd once had her heart and broken it, that she'd felt like this about him once before and he'd tossed her out of his life and moved on. If she and Beck slept together, she knew her feelings for him would deepen but his wouldn't. He didn't want what she did and she'd be the one to end up hurt. She'd have to pick her beaten and battered heart up from off the floor.

He'd love her, physically, but she knew the day would come when it would end and she had to protect herself. She could not allow herself to fall in love with him. If she did, and he stabbed her heart again, she feared that she would never recover.

No, it was better that she keep her very desperate hands to herself.

"Hey, Cady, where's Driven?" Linc demanded from across the room.

"Who?" Cady asked, lowering her arm.

"Beck," Sage explained, taking the spare seat next to her. "Linc and Jay have called him that since he was a kid. Because he works so damn hard."

The nickname was apt, Cady admitted. Beck did work ridiculously long hours.

"Oh. I don't know," she told Linc.

"I'll call him," Jaeger said and whipped out his phone. He walked through the front door and into the hallway and laughed. "Hey, we were just talking about you."

"And don't you look like a pretty boy with your perfect stubble and styled hair."

Cady heard Beck's drawl, and her stomach tightened. She turned her head to look over the back of the couch and sent him a small smile. A frown appeared between Beck's eyebrows as he took off his coat. "Hi. You okay?"

Cady started to answer but Shaw hit his knees with the force of a tiny tank, so she just nodded. Beck tossed Shaw into the air, and the noise level increased again. Cady thought her head might explode.

The mayhem continued as Jose and his crew said their goodbyes. After they left, Cady sat down again and closed her eyes. She felt Beck's hand on her shoulder and when she opened her eyes, she saw that he held two pills in his hand and a glass of water. She lifted her eyes to his and shook her head. She couldn't explain that she couldn't take anything because of the baby. Not in front of everyone.

"These are safe," Beck assured her, his voice pitched low enough so that only she could hear him. "Trust me."

She did. And that was the problem. She couldn't afford to.

Cady swallowed her pills and turned her head as Piper sat down next to her. "The boys are ordering pizza. Stay and eat with us."

"I should get home," Cady said, although she didn't have the energy to move.

"Stay," Piper urged her. "It'll be here in twenty minutes. Have a slice and I'll order a cab to take you home."

She could be home within forty-five minutes. A bath, her bed. Bliss. But for now she had to try to be sociable.

She thanked Piper for the invitation and nodded at the gorgeous sapphire on Piper's ring finger. It was the same ring that Jaeger had held and posed with all afternoon. "It's a stunning ring."

"I love it," Piper said, her voice full of emotion.

"I designed it," Sage said from across the room. There was pride in her voice and Cady realized that the Ballantynes, for the first time that evening, were all tuned in to the same conversation. "It's one of my favorite designs," Sage added.

"It should be since it was a special commission and you charged me through the nose for it," Jaeger grumbled. "Linc stiffed me on the cost of the stone and you wiped out my bank account with the price of your design."

Piper laughed at him. "Good thing you live rent free with me. I'd hate to see you homeless and begging. And, as you keep forgetting, Sage said that the design was our engagement present."

"Is it?" Jaeger's face brightened. "Cool."

"Actually, it was my way to thank Piper for taking you off our hands," Sage teased. "But if you want to pay me, you can."

"I can't afford you." He continued the joke by looking at Linc and raising his eyebrows. "How about giving Piper the sapphire as a thank-you for marrying me, too?"

"I love Piper but not that much," Linc replied, his tone dry. "Nice try, though."

Sage raised her eyebrows at Cady. "As you can see, I'm happy to pay the price to be rid of my annoying brothers. Are you interested in making a deal?"

Oh, God, yes, right now. She'd take Beck off her

hands, into her hands. She really wanted him in her hands... God knew how much longer she could resist him. A day? An hour? Ten more minutes?

An awkward silence fell over the room, and Cady wondered if her thoughts were on her face. Blushing, she decided the only way to defuse the tension was to crack a joke. "Sure, I'll take Linc off your hands." She grinned at Beck's scowl and nodded at Sage. "Let's negotiate."

"Let's not," Beck muttered, placing his hand on her shoulder as if to stake his claim.

Sage and Piper exchanged a long look and they both nodded. "Quick and smart," Sage commented. "We like you. If you stick, I'll up my offer."

If she stuck... No chance of that happening.

Eight

An hour later and back in her apartment, south of Jaeger and Piper's red Victorian in Park Slope, Beck took Cady's coat and hung it up, trying to suppress the urge to jump her. It had been hell trying to keep his mouth, hands and other parts of his body to himself and he was running out of patience. Tonight he didn't think he could.

Maybe it had something to do with her fitting into his family, her easy banter with his sister, the way she looked at him across the room. It might be one or all of the above but mostly it was because she was all feminine heat, creamy skin, desire and deliciousness, and he couldn't go one more night without finding out if she was as good as he remembered. He had to have her.

"Shall I make coffee, Beck? Would you like some?"

Beck turned to face her and noticed that she'd slipped out of her heels, holding them so that they dangled by their ankle straps. Her lipstick was gone and a curl had escaped from the bundled, sexy mess on her head and she looked glad to be home.

Her sexy factor nearly dropped him to the floor.

Beck just stared at her, knowing that his eyes, the look on his face and the rod in his pants would tell her exactly what he wanted, and it sure as hell wasn't coffee.

Cady's eyes darkened, her nipples tightened and she shifted her weight from one foot to the other as if trying to escape the heat between her thighs. There was no escape, they had to go there and it was inevitable. It had been since the moment he saw her in the hallway at Ballantyne International.

"I'm *pregnant*, Beck," she reminded him, as if that had any bearing on the situation.

He shook his head and jammed his hands into the pockets of his suit pants to keep them from reaching for her. "So? I look at you and I stop breathing and all I can think about is getting you into my bed, hearing your moans, slipping inside you to see if you feel as good as I remember."

"Beck…"

"Tell me that you want me, Cady." He wasn't going to move toward her until he heard her say the words.

Cady dropped her shoes to the floor and moved toward him, as graceful as a prima ballerina. She pushed her hand under the lapel of his suit jacket and through his cotton dress shirt, her hand burning his skin. "I've thought of you, imagined touching you. You are so hard, Beck. Your chest, your stomach…" Her eyes dropped to the tent in his pants. "Everywhere."

Cady pushed his jacket off his shoulders and he allowed it to fall down his arms and onto the floor. It was designer but hell, who cared? Cady was touching him and that was all that mattered. She pulled his tie off and undid the button at his neck, and resting her hands on his chest, she rose on her tiptoes and placed a warm, openmouthed kiss at the base of his neck. Beck felt heat and electricity shoot down his spine and tighten his balls.

"Tell me, Cady."

"I want you, Beck."

That was what he wanted—no, needed—to hear. He yanked her into him, pressing her breasts against his chest. He dropped his head and at the same time, she lifted her mouth and they fused together, their mouths clashing and tongues dueling. Her tongue swirled around his and memory collided with reality. What they shared now was even better than he remembered. Cady made a sexy sound in her throat, and her fingers dug into his chest.

She tasted of the crisp winter air and longing, and kissing her was both a comforting memory and a fresh pleasure. Her perfume swirled up from her heated skin and her scent, lemongrass and jasmine, took him back to the hot Thailand nights by the sea.

He hiked up her shirt so he had access to her creamy skin. Still kissing her, unable to pull away, he placed one arm below her butt and yanked her up and into him. Her legs, as he knew they would, opened and curled around his waist. But that contact was not enough. Still needing more, he pushed her down so that she brushed his erection with her mound. When her kisses turned fiercer and she ground against him, he realized that the passion between them was hotter than before, deeper, all grown up.

Beck walked her over to the kitchen counter and set her down on the cool surface, still standing between her legs and feeling her heat radiating from her core. He cradled her face, tipping her head to change the angle so that he had easy access to every part of her mouth. Cady's moans of approval sent the last droplets of blood from his brain to points south and he strained the fabric on the front of his pants.

She was sex and heat and sweetness and softness and he needed her. So much more than he should. He couldn't stop, didn't want to stop. This train had left the station but he had to slow it down. He didn't want to take her on the kitchen counter. After so long, he needed to be in a bed. He wanted to take his time to rediscover her, to explore every inch of her endlessly sexy skin.

Although he didn't want to, Beck pulled his mouth from hers to rest his chin in her hair. "Cady."

She muttered something unintelligible as he felt her lips flutter against his skin.

"We need to slow down," he told her. "Find some more room."

"Trust me, my bed is not much bigger than this counter," Cady muttered. "Don't stop, Beck."

"I want to take it slow."

"Next time."

She'd barely finished her sentence when his mouth captured hers. Her words gave him permission to lose control, the control he was so famous for. With Cady, his brain shut down and biology took over. As her tongue met his swipe for swipe, he lifted her shirt over her head and immediately noticed that she wasn't wearing a bra. He thumbed her already hard nipple and Cady pushed her breast into his touch, silently demanding more. She ran her fingers across his taut stomach, stopping now and again to make a swirling motion as she let them drift lower before settling them on his erection.

He couldn't wait much longer. He needed her, needed to be inside her.

Beck wrenched his mouth off hers and attacked the button of her pants, sliding her zipper down. "Lift up," he ordered her and Cady lifted her butt, allowing him to pull the slacks down her slim thighs. The garment dropped to the floor and he kicked it aside.

He leaned back and sucked in a breath, taking a moment to appreciate her rosy nipples, her endlessly creamy skin, the barrier of pale pink lace over her feminine mound. He lifted his eyes to her flushed face and his voice was low and harsh when he spoke. "Here? Now?"

"Here. Now."

Beck used one hand to pull his shirt over his head and the other to pull his wallet out of the back pocket of his pants. He tossed it into her lap. "There's a condom somewhere in there."

While Cady searched his wallet with trembling fingers, he stepped out of his shoes and hastily undressed, till he stood naked between her warm thighs.

He put on the condom she held out to him, then hooked his hands under the backs of her knees and pulled her to him so that his tip probed her entrance. She felt so good.

He really wanted to take her to bed, or the floor, somewhere where he could really look at her, feel every inch of her as he entered her. "Cady, we are not doing this on the kitchen counter."

Cady touched her mouth to his before speaking. "If you make me move, I swear I will punch you. I need you, Beck. Make me whole," she murmured against his lips.

Beck groaned and pushed into her, sighing when her tongue echoed his action and slid into his mouth. An inch, then one more, and another and he was inside her. Cady pushed her heels into his back, asking for more, and within seconds Beck was buried to the hilt.

Yeah, he missed this. He missed her.

"God, Beck, you feel so good," Cady said, burying her face into his neck. "Take me over the edge, Beck. You know how. You always did."

Beck surged into her and slid a finger between

them, stroking her, and around him he felt Cady
tense. He could feel her orgasm hovering, so he
rocked into her one more time and she shattered
around him.

Then, with a hoarse, relieved cry, he followed her
into that fireball.

Another day, another photo shoot. Another day
of trying to work out what, exactly, was bubbling
between her and Beck. Since she'd barely spent any
time with him since her amazing night with him
four days ago, she couldn't take her cue from Beck.
Panty-dissolving sex aside, Cady thought, nothing,
essentially, had changed. He was still her boss; she
was still pregnant; she had a job to do, a business to
save, to grow.

Cady watched Emma, the photographer's assistant, carry a small ladder out Beck's door and Beck
closed the door to the loft behind her. A dozen people had filled this space an hour before—stylists,
makeup artists and creative directors. Now only she
and Beck remained. Cady sat on the third step of
Beck's wide spiral staircase, her computer on her
knees, looking through the photographs Jose wire-
lessly transmitted to her device.

Like his siblings had in their photos, Beck wore
a designer white dress shirt, collar open and cuffs
rolled up his arms. His jeans were faded from years
of washing, and the fabric clung to his narrow hips
and long legs, and he wore no shoes. She scrolled
through the shots, pleased that they conveyed the

exact image she was going for in the campaign: the rich, successful, super-sexy Ballantyne siblings at ease in their homes or, in Sage's case, in her studio.

They looked young and smart, aspirational and accessible. Cady knew that the print ads would make the rich millennials sit up and take notice.

She stopped on a photograph of Beck sitting exactly where she was, his knees apart and holding the fake copy of his mom's ring between his finger and thumb, looking at the camera, his eyes deep and mysterious. His broody attitude, wide shoulders and the brilliance of the pink-red stone screamed class. And cool.

As with his siblings' ads, consumers were encouraged to read the story behind the piece of jewelry on the website, and that would link them to Sage's latest hip and sleek collection. They'd already released Jaeger's and Sage's ads, and Linc's was due to be released tomorrow, Beck's later in the week. The Ballantyne website had never received so many hits.

Cady felt a flutter of excitement as she marked the photo. She looked up when Beck, holding a cup of coffee, took his seat next to her. "Can I drink this here next to you? Or are you going to bolt for the bathroom?"

Her morning sickness wasn't a constant presence, just triggered by sights and smells. The smell of chicken sent her running, as did vanilla. Sometimes coffee was her friend, sometimes her foe. Cady took a tentative sniff, waited a little while and when her stomach didn't react, she smiled. "Today is a good coffee day."

Beck pressed his shoulder into hers and looked at the screen. "Is that the shot you want to use?"

Cady nodded. "But you can look through the others if you'd like to."

"Hell, no, I trust you. Damn, this thing is poking a hole in my skin." Beck leaned back, pulled the copy of his mom's ring out of the front pocket of his jeans and rested it on his knee. Cady moved her laptop to the floor and picked up the ring, examining it in the fading light of the late afternoon.

"It's so beautiful, Beck."

"And it's only a fake. The real one is deeper, more vibrant, the color more intense." Beck sipped his coffee. "Her ring is my first memory, that and her smell."

"Tell me about her." Cady twisted to face him, her knees against his thigh.

Beck put his hand on her knee and kept his eyes on the ring she held. "I remember her hand over mine. I was holding a crayon. We're both left-handed so that's why I remember the ring. I was so young but I remember being fascinated by the color."

"American rose," Cady murmured, allowing the stone to catch the light. "It's a shade of red, between red and magenta…and it's called American rose. I wished I could've seen the real deal," Cady murmured.

"Yeah, I wouldn't mind seeing the ring, and them, again," Beck said, his voice threaded with pain. "Unfortunately both are in pieces on that mountain in Vermont."

Cady changed position so that she could thread her arm through Beck's and hold his hand. "I'm sorry, Beck. God, you were all so young."

"Yeah. Ten, eight and six." Beck's coffee cup shook as he lifted it to his lips. "I still miss them."

"I think you always will," Cady said, keeping her voice low. This was the first time Beck ever talked about his past and his parents, and she didn't want to break the spell by talking too much or by saying the wrong thing.

Beck stared at his bare feet, pale against the laminated floor. "My siblings missed out on so much. Their parents weren't at Jaeger's games, their graduations, Sage's ballet concerts. My father won't walk Sage down the aisle. Ty and Shaw won't go with my dad to find semiprecious gems like we did." Beck rubbed his jaw and pushed his hand to the back of his neck.

He never once mentioned himself, what he'd like to do with his parents, she noticed. "And what did you miss out on, not having your parents there?"

Silence, hot and heavy, hung between them, and Cady wondered if he would reply to her question. She saw him pull in a deep breath as he turned his eyes to her. They were saturated with pain. "It doesn't matter what I missed out on. It never did."

Whoa. What?

Cady frowned, opened her mouth to loudly object to his statement and saw the misery on his face. He hadn't said that lightly. He meant every cruel and bitter word. After squeezing his hand, she carefully chose her next words. "Beck, why would you think that? You lost your parents, too."

"But it was my fault they died."

Cady felt the words slam into her, stopping her breath and paralyzing her vocal cords. When her brain restarted, she noticed that Beck was in the process of rising to his feet, intending to walk away. Oh, hell, no. He was going to sit here and talk this through. He'd been eight, for God's sake; no eight-year-old was responsible for his parents' deaths. It was sheer luck that Cady managed to snag a belt loop through his shirt but she did and she pulled him back down. "Sit down."

Beck shook his head. "I have a report to write, some financials to go through."

"You need to sit here and talk to me," Cady hotly replied. Beck sighed and sat and looked mutinous. She stared at his stone-like profile and shook her head. "Why would you think that, Beck?"

"Because that's what happened. Cady, I don't want to talk about this."

She ignored the second part of his statement. "No, that's not what happened! I know that you were at The Den with your uncle and your siblings so you didn't do anything to cause their deaths. So what do you mean?" She wished she could reach into him and yank his words out.

Beck cursed and muttered something about him having a big mouth. He raked his hand through his hair and sighed, then eventually, reluctantly, he answered her. "I broke my wrist skateboarding and it wasn't a straight break. It needed to be pinned and I had to have an operation. I was petrified. I'd watched a horror movie that took place in a hospital and I was convinced that the zombies would get me, and Jaeger was egging on my fears. I asked my folks to come home, to be with me. I was crying on the phone, practically hysterical, and they decided to fly home right away. The weather was bad and my dad took a chance. The weather closed in and he didn't have enough height to clear that mountain."

His dad took a chance, she wanted to point out to him, not him. He'd just been a kid asking for his parents. Why would he think he was at fault? "I still don't understand why you think their crashing is your fault. Your dad gambled and lost."

"At the reception after the funeral, I heard a conversation between two people I knew. They said it was my fault, that a broken arm is a hell of a price to pay for the deaths of two amazing people."

"Oh, Beckett."

"And they also mentioned that my mom was pregnant. We had a sibling on the way so I was responsible for the loss of three lives."

Swamped with anger for the young boy Beckett had been, Cady moved to stand between his open legs and wrapped her fists in his shirt. She waited until he looked into her eyes and when he did, she took a breath and then another, to get her temper under control. When she spoke she heard her burning fury in her words. "The insensitive bastards! What they said was *wrong*, Beck! Wrong and *ugly*!

"Who were they?" she demanded, her anger bubbling in the back of her throat.

"Why?" Beck asked, confused.

"Because I swear I will track them down and strip fifty layers off them. How dare they say that? How dare they!"

Beck pulled on her wrists and she realized that his shirt was tight against his chest and a good portion of it was wrapped around her hands. She released the fabric and placed her hands on Beck's shoulders.

"Cady, I appreciate your anger on my behalf but it was a long time ago."

Cady shushed him to keep quiet and closed her eyes in an attempt to harness her anger. It wasn't often that she lost her temper. It didn't matter that they were two faceless, nameless people whom he'd last seen almost twenty-five years ago; they'd hurt him to the depths of his soul. Nobody hurt Beck, not like that.

She waited a moment until she thought she could speak again then opened her eyes. Beck was looking at her, looking awed and confused.

"You okay?" he asked her.

"Yeah," Cady replied. She felt him start to move and she pushed her hands down, trying to keep him in place. "Where do you think you're going?"

"I was going to take my cup to the kitchen and then I was going to do some work, since I lost the afternoon staring into the camera."

"Oh, hell, no, you're not." Cady shook her head. She pushed his legs together and straddled him, taking his rough, stubbled, beautiful face in her hands.

Beck managed a small smile but his eyes reflected only desolation. "Or we can go to bed. I vote for that."

"That's not in the cards, either, or at least not right now." Cady swiped her thumb across his bottom lip. "Right now I am going to talk and you are going to listen."

Beck narrowed his eyes and she felt him pull away from her. His fingers on her hips pushed into her skin as if to warn her to change the subject. He could glower and glare at her all he liked; he needed to hear what she had to say.

"I can't force you to listen to me, Beck, but I hope you will."

Beck muttered a curse and she saw his resentment and under that, his fear. To his credit, and her surprise, he stayed where he was.

"Beck, you are not responsible," Cady told him, keeping her voice low but allowing her sincerity to be heard. "You were a scared kid and you had every right to ask your parents to come home to be with you. And they, being the parents they were, heard your plea and made their way home. That's what good parents do."

"But—"

"Your dad took a chance, and it worked out badly. It wasn't your fault," Cady insisted.

"She was pregnant, Cades!"

"And they could've died in a car accident and her being pregnant and them dying wouldn't be your fault either. You were eight. You wanted and needed your parents, and there is no need for you to feel guilty. None, Beck." Cady's eyes filled with tears. "Intellectually, you know this."

"Yeah, but—"

"No buts." Cady felt a tear roll down her cheek and she sniffed. "Please don't do this to yourself."

Beck's hand moved from her hip to her face, tracing her jawline with his fingers, his touch sparking wherever he touched. "My siblings still don't know that she was pregnant. Should I—"

"Tell them?" Cady finished his sentence for him. "I don't know, Beck. But maybe it's a way to start dismantling that suit of armor between you and your siblings, you and the world."

"I don't—" Beck started, half laughed and shook his head. "Yeah, I do wear that armor. You always had the ability to find my weak spots and sneak on in. Cades, you…this…"

Cady stopped his fumbling words with her lips on his. She didn't want him to say more, to make promises he couldn't keep just because he was feeling emotional. This entire interlude was too intense and she had to pull away now because she couldn't fall any deeper into whatever was building between her and Beck.

Too much had happened lately; too much was at stake. She was, for the second time, sleeping with a client and although Beck said that he could, and would, separate the two issues, she'd been burned in this situation before. She was pregnant and Beck wasn't the father and they didn't have a future.

She wasn't going to fall in love with Beck again. It didn't matter that he was the best man she'd ever met, that she thought he was sexy as sin, that she adored him.

This. Was. Not. Going. To. Happen.

She was not going to fall in love with Beck. Not again.

"Let's go to bed." Beck's hot chocolate voice rumbled over her.

She shook her head and stood in front of him.

Beck frowned at her. "Problem?" Beck asked, concern in his voice.

Cady shot steel into her spine and told herself to be sensible. "Having sex after such an intense conversation is not a good idea."

"Having sex is always a good idea," Beck argued.

Such a man answer, Cady thought. "No, it's *not*. Emotions get jumbled up with physical pleasure, and everything gets turned upside down. We're emotionally connected at the moment and that could deepen if we sleep together. It's better that we take some time, put some space between us."

Beck took a minute to answer her. "And that would be a bad thing?"

"Of course it would be a bad thing! Beck, you broke my heart and I'm not prepared to give you another chance to do that. I'm working for you and I am being so damn unprofessional. I hate myself for not being able to resist you. And, for God's sake, just to add to this pile of crazy, I'm pregnant!"

"Your being pregnant isn't a problem for me," Beck said, his eyes hot but his voice calm.

"It should be!" Cady threw her hands up in the air at his stubborn face. "I'm hormonal, emotional and I know myself well enough to know that sex with you, right now, would not be good for me." Cady couldn't blink away the tears in her eyes. "I need some distance, Beck. From you, from us, from how you make me feel."

"Why?"

Cady picked up her laptop, shoved it into her tote bag and did a quick scan of his loft for anything she'd left behind.

"Because I don't want to get too used to something I know is temporary. Because one of these days you're going to get scared and bolt and I can't allow you to break my heart again. I can handle sex with you, I can handle being friends with you, I can work for you—but I can't be emotionally attached to you. I can't let you break my heart again, Beck."

Cady walked to the door and put her hand on the knob and pulled it open.

"Cady."

She looked over her shoulder to see him standing there, hot and a little bewildered. "Yeah?"

"My heart broke, too."

Cady lifted one shoulder in a sad shrug. "That was your choice, Beck, not mine."

Nine

"Come on, guys," Beck complained as he stepped out of the taxi in front of The Den, the brownstone he'd grown up in. He scowled at the paparazzi standing in front of the steps leading up to the front door. "Isn't there someone else for you to stalk?"

A bearded man in a combat jacket shrugged and lifted his camera to his face. "You and Cady are the current fascination. When are you going to admit or deny your engagement?"

"When hell freezes over," Beck retorted, holding his hand out to Cady. Her bare fingers slid into his hand and he felt the same buzz he always did when they connected. They'd been sleeping together for more than two weeks and the electricity arcing between them seemed to be intensifying. As if by mutual agreement they kept the sex between them hot, the conversation light. Damn him for, occasionally, wanting the sex to be fun and the conversation deep. But, he acknowledged, it was safer this way.

Cady climbed out of the cab and immediately buried her face in her voluminous scarf. A hat covered her dark curls and she looked mysterious and sexy, and Beck knew that the media's interest in her was fueled in part because she was an unknown and because she looked liked Audrey Hepburn with light eyes and long hair.

"When is the wedding?"

Beck ignored the question and pulled a shivering Cady to his side as they walked up the steps to the imposing front door of The Den.

"Cady isn't wearing your mom's ring. Why not?"

Because it's fake, you moron, and no fiancée of mine is going to wear a fake engagement ring.

"None of your business." Beck tossed the words over his shoulder. Nobody outside the family knew what happened to the original ring, the real one. He'd looked but he hadn't found another stone to match it. Red beryl was incredibly rare and stones above two and three carats were even rarer. Finding another five-carat beauty was impossible.

It didn't matter; he was never going to offer it to a woman—Cady or anybody else.

He unlocked the door and ushered Cady inside, inhaling the familiar smell of fresh flowers and beeswax polish. He took off his coat, hung it up on the rack next to the door and watched Cady unwind her scarf.

She looked nervous and he couldn't blame her. His family would all be present tonight, including Amy and Tate, who'd moved into The Den with her sister's—and Linc's ex-fiancée's—ten-month-old baby. What was with all the babies suddenly? Up until three months ago there had only been Shaw, Linc's four-year-old, but now they were being over-run with the smaller species. Ty was new, Linc's ex's baby was living with them, Piper was pregnant and Cady was pregnant.

Was there something in the water?

Beck took Cady's coat and scarf and noted how beautiful she looked She wore a tight-fitting blue sweater over a blue-and-white-checked shirt, equally tight camel-colored jeans tucked into brown, knee-high leather boots. She didn't need designer clothes to look stylish; she had a way of putting together outfits that just worked. Unlike him. He needed a stylist to buy his clothes. Stefan even packed his closet, hanging all the items together so that Beck couldn't go wrong.

Cady jumped at the shout of laughter coming from the living room, and Beck took her hand. "It'll be okay, Cady. This is a safe place. You don't need to pretend here."

"Then why am I here?" Cady asked. "I don't need to be here."

Her lack of enthusiasm about spending time with his family shouldn't hurt him but it did. These were his people, dammit, and he wanted her to like them. And them to like her. But why? he asked himself. It wasn't like she was going to be a permanent part of his life.

Irritated with his irrational thoughts, Beck said, "You haven't had time to brief Linc, Sage and Jaeger about the response to the campaign. They don't know what a success it's been. I thought you could do that tonight."

"But you try not to talk business at these dinners," Cady replied.

"We try not to but we always do. It's a hazard of running a family business." He grabbed her hand and pulled her to him. "What's the matter, Cades?"

Her eyes skittered away from his. "Do they know I'm pregnant?" she asked.

"I haven't told them."

"Why not?"

"Because it has nothing to do with them. But if you want to tell them, feel free."

Cady shook her head. "No, I just thought you would've—"

"I didn't," Beck assured her. When she still wouldn't look at him, he asked, "What else is bugging you, Cady?"

"I'm not usually intimidated by people, regardless of how rich they are, but this—you—" Cady waved her hand around the hall "—this is serious, Beckett."

Serious? What was serious? "You've lost me."

"The Ballantynes are old money New York, one of the most influential families in the city. I'm from a middle-class family in a tiny upstate town. This house, the business… It's all a bit intimidating, Beck. The chandelier, the staircase, the fancy furniture."

"The hall table is eighteenth century. French, I think, but my grandmother found it in a junk shop and restored it herself." He looked up at the massive chandelier. "If you look carefully, there are still tiny spitballs on it. It was a prime target when we were kids. Yeah, the staircase is imposing but hell, you can get some serious speed when you slide down the banister on your butt. It's just a house, Cady."

"Cool! Can I do that, Uncle Beck?"

Beck turned and saw blonde-haired and blue-eyed Shaw standing next to him. The kid had skills that ninjas didn't, Beck thought, hoisting the kid up and over his shoulder to dangle him down his back, his hand gripping both his ankles.

"Beckett!" Cady gasped, shocked.

"Don't worry, he always does this," Shaw told her, laughter in his voice.

Beck fumbled his grip, trying to scare the boy, but Shaw just giggled. "Nice try, Uncle Beck. I know you won't drop me, because if you do my dad will fry your gizzards in hot oil."

"Do you even know what a gizzard is?" Cady asked him, amused.

"Nope. I'm Shaw, who are you?" Shaw asked as Beckett started to walk in the direction of the living room.

"I'm Cady."

Beck stood back to gesture her into the room that

held the crew. Jo, Linc's mom, held a cute biracial, blue-eyed baby, and Ty, Jaeger's son, was sitting between Jaeger's feet on the floor and dropping biscuit crumbs on the rare Persian carpet. Piper was talking to Amy, and Linc was watching Tate, who stood apart from the family, looking like she was ready to bolt.

Fun times at The Den, Beck thought on a wry smile.

As his brothers stood up, Shaw wiggled his way into Beck's arms. The boy stared at him, clearly puzzled. "The storks must be really busy at the moment, hey, Uncle Beck?"

Storks? Had Shaw moved on from his train craze to birds? "Why do you say that, bud?"

"Well," Shaw said into the silence that had fallen over the room, "storks bring babies and there have been a lot of them lately. There's Ty and Ellie, and Piper has a baby in her tummy and Cady said she's pregnant—that means she has a baby in her tummy, too, doesn't it?"

Oh, dammithellcrap. All the curse words Jo banned from this house came rushing through his mind as one.

Thanks, Shaw, Beck thought as Cady turned pale and bolted for the powder room.

Thanks a lot, buddy.

Beck turned back to his family and sighed at their raised eyebrows, their cocked heads. He also caught the resignation on his siblings' faces, the expectation that he would refuse to discuss this any further. It was what he did, as Cady had pointed out to him the other night when she'd cried tears for the little boy he'd been.

He'd thought long and hard about what she'd said, and her belief in his innocence melted some of the ice around his heart, the guilt he'd lived with all his life. For the first time in forever, he thought that maybe it was time to forgive the child he'd been. Oh, he wasn't there yet but maybe, with a little work, he could get there one day soon.

But he did know that it was time to really start reconnecting with his family, that he needed to start opening up to them on a deeper level. These were the people he trusted and it was time he showed them that he did. He took the glass of whiskey Jaeger poured for him and shrugged. "It's not my kid."

He thought he should clear that up, just in case anyone had their doubts.

"We kind of figured that," Linc drawled.

"Yeah, you work fast but not that fast," Jaeger added.

Piper smacked her fiancé's shoulder and sent him a "be serious" glare. Beck tossed her a look of gratitude. Opening up and talking was hard enough as it was without having to deal with their sarcasm. "How far along is she, Beck?" Piper asked.

Beck shrugged, embarrassed that he didn't know. "I'm not sure."

"Beckett, really?" Jo asked, shocked.

"Has she seen a doctor?"

"Is she taking vitamins? Getting enough sleep?"

Amy, Julia, Piper and even Tate looked horrified at his lack of information. But, in his defense, every time he raised the issue of her pregnancy, Cady changed the subject. He hadn't pushed and if the looks he was receiving from the females in his life were to be believed, he'd messed up, big-time.

"Is her being pregnant a problem for you?" Amy demanded.

Beckett frowned. "What do you mean?"

"If you're developing feelings for her, will her pregnancy put you off?"

He looked down the hall to make sure that Cady hadn't left the powder room. "I'm *not* developing feelings for her, Ames."

Or was he?

She was the only one he'd ever told his whole story to, the only one who knew about his mother's pregnancy. She occupied far too many of his daytime thoughts and his nighttime dreams. Being with her, making love to her, was the closest thing to heaven on earth.

Or maybe it was just the residual feelings from years ago seeping their way back into his psyche. It didn't mean that he was in love with her.

He couldn't be. It wasn't part of his life plan.

A life plan he'd made for himself at eight? How reasonable was that?

Beck frowned at that rogue thought and shook his head, quickly turning back to the conversation at hand. He'd rather take grief from his family than consider that he'd based his life on a lie.

"You didn't answer the question." Sage leaned forward, her eyes on his. "Would Cady being pregnant with someone else's child be a problem for you?"

If he decided to be with Cady, would a baby be a problem? He didn't think so. He liked kids, babies didn't scare him and he could, thanks to babysitting Shaw more times than he could remember, do what needed to be done. And yeah, he wasn't thrilled that she was pregnant by someone else, but if the choice was between Cady and baby or no Cady, he knew that he'd chose her and the child.

But that wasn't a choice he was going to make.

He lifted his glass in Linc's direction. "Linc's not blood but we seem to like him enough. If I decided to take on a woman with a child who wasn't mine, I'd probably feel the same."

"Are you thinking of taking her on?" Linc demanded. "Because if you're not, then you've got to let this go, Beck, before she gets hurt."

Beck shook his head. "Whoa, hold on. I'm not the only one who has his foot on the brake. She's equally wary, equally not willing to start something we can't finish."

"You really hurt her before, Beck. Please don't do it again," Sage begged him.

Beck heard the door to the powder room open and he made a slashing motion across his face to silently order his family to change the subject. As he watched Cady walk back toward him, he thought it ironic that his family was so damned worried about her.

Not one of them thought of the emotional danger he was in. None of them considered that his heart was on the line, as well. Was he that removed, that blasé, that they thought he couldn't be hurt?

They really didn't know him at all. And whose fault was that? His. They'd tried; he hadn't. He was the only person to blame.

Right, that had to be changed.

Waking up in Beck's bed the morning after the dinner with his family, which she'd enjoyed more than she should have, Cady heard the shower going in the en suite bathroom. Scooting up, she leaned her back against his leather headboard and pushed her tangled hair off her face. They'd made love last night and she'd fallen into a deep, dreamless sleep, wrapped in Beck's arms. She loved spending time with him and, because her place was the size of a shoe box and Beck was a big man, they tended to gravitate to his place. As a result, Cady was starting to feel far too at home in his loft and his life.

She just had to get through the cocktail party and exhibition of the Ballantyne jewelry collection and then her contract would be over. She had some money in the bank and better yet, a contract to do PR for a minor-league baseball team and another for a celebrity chef who was launching his own line of cookware. Between Julia's recommendations and the fact that the Ballantyne International campaign was a huge success, she now had clients knocking on her door. With the money she earned from Ballantyne's and these new contracts, she could rehire some of her staff and run a functioning office again.

She was back in business.

The Ballantyne contract would end next week and neither she, nor Beck, had broached the subject of whether they would continue to see each other after that. It was better if they didn't, Cady admitted.

She could no longer pretend that she wasn't pregnant. Her stomach and breasts were rapidly expanding, and it was time for her to walk away from Beck before she started to show. Her being pregnant would raise a lot of interest in the press and she'd have to admit that the baby wasn't Beck's, which would make her look flaky at best, or, at worst, like someone who bed-hopped from one boss's bed to another.

An even better reason to walk away from Beck was because she wanted this; she wanted him. Oh, not the luxurious loft or the designer furniture but what it represented. Security, companionship, acceptance...

Love.

She wanted him to love her. She'd thought she wanted him at nineteen but it didn't come close to the depth of what she now felt. Back then she'd a vague idea of life with Beck but that was a life on the road, slightly unreal. Life with Beck, grown-up life, meant early-morning coffee after he came in from the gym, sex in the shower, arguing about politics—she was a little conservative, he a tad too liberal—sharing meals, time, memories and their bodies.

With Beck she felt alive, like the real, genuine Cady she'd always wanted to be.

But she was pregnant, he was her boss and he didn't want her the way she wanted him. One of

these days, when the bloom left the rose, he'd realize that he was in too deep and he'd back off, all the
way off. And he'd let her go. Could she live her life
wondering whether this was the day, the hour, the
minute he'd decide that it wasn't working, that it was
time for her to go?

If he left, she couldn't crawl up into a ball and sob.
She had a business to run, a child to raise.

This time her heart wouldn't break, it would shat-
ter. And she'd have no hope of patching it together
again.

It would be better if she gently, quietly, put some
distance between them. She'd spend less time with
him and in a month or two, they could issue a quiet
press statement saying that they'd parted amicably
and were still good friends.

Cady's head snapped up as the bathroom door
opened and Beck stepped out, a towel wrapped
around his waist and droplets of water still on
his chest and arms. His eyes widened in what she
thought might be pleasure at seeing her still in his
bed. "Hi. You're awake. Sleep well?"

Cady nodded. She watched as he dried his hair
with a small towel and slung it around his neck.

He walked to his closet and within seconds he
was back, with a hanger holding a complete outfit.
Tawny-colored pants, a white shirt and a dark gray
jacket. He tossed the outfit on the bed and she saw a
tag showing a complete list of every item, including
shoes. She recognized the logo on the card as that of
one of the city's best and most discreet men's stylists.

Cady grinned. Beck did not have fabulous taste as she first suspected; he just had a great stylist. Thinking that she could mess with him, she tipped her head to the side.

"I think a navy jacket would look better than the gray."

Beck looked at the outfit, looked at her and back at the outfit. Panic crossed his face. "Uh... I don't think so."

"The gray is a bit dull. I think it needs some punch, a red pullover, maybe orange?" She couldn't help her grin and Beck caught it.

He grabbed the wet towel from his neck and threw it with deadly accuracy right at her face. "Brat."

Cady pulled the towel off her face, laughing as she threw it back at him. "You are so spoiled! I thought you had great taste in clothes but it's Stefan's."

"It is my taste, sort of." Beck flicked the towel at her leg. "Initially, for every ten outfits Stefan chose, I'd only wear one, the most conservative one. He now knows what I will and will not wear."

"Why don't you just choose your own clothes?" Cady demanded.

"Shopping?" Beck shuddered. "Shoot me. Besides, I really do have crap taste. I'd go to work in faded jeans and flannel shirts if I had the choice."

He sat down on the edge of the bed, his butt next to her thigh, and placed his hands on either side of her body, caging her in. He looked serious, his jaw tense. "We need to talk."

Cady nodded. Maybe this was it; maybe he was

about to tell her that it was time they walked away. He'd be gentle with her; he wouldn't be as abrupt as last time. He'd explain why he thought it better that they part and she'd agree and she wouldn't cry.

She wouldn't. Okay, she'd try not to.

"We've avoided the subject of your pregnancy, mostly because you've ducked the subject every time I've raised it."

Pregnancy? He wanted to talk about that? Cady pulled her head back to look at him, utterly confounded. "You want to talk about my baby?" she clarified.

"Yeah. And you're not going anywhere until you answer my questions."

Oh, God, he wasn't breaking it off! Her relief made her feel light-headed and she grabbed Beck's thigh to ground herself.

"How far along are you, Cady?"

Flustered, Cady had to think hard to answer that question. "Twelve, thirteen weeks?"

"Have you seen a doctor?" Beck asked.

Cady shook her head. "I've been meaning to but I've been quite busy, you know, trying to run a successful campaign."

Beck didn't react to her peevish tone. "And the father? Will you tell me who he is?"

"Does it matter?"

Cady saw impatience in Beck's eyes at her evasive response and she sighed, lifting her hand from his thigh. "He's not interested in me or the baby."

"Is he going to pay any of your medical expenses, support the kid when it comes along?"

"No." Cady snapped the word out.

"Cady, I'm not the enemy and I don't want to pull this out of you. Talk to me."

She lifted her arms and cradled her head. "It doesn't matter, Beck," she cried. "I'm doing this solo."

"It does matter. Talk."

Cady dropped her arms and stared past Beck's shoulder. She'd talk, but she'd keep it short. "He's married. I didn't realize until I told him I was pregnant. He lied to me, told me he was divorced. He wanted me to have an abortion. He's not prepared to pay child support."

"Douche."

Cady's eyes flew to his face and she saw his anger, not at but for her. Underneath the anger, she saw support and empathy and understanding. If she was going to tell him everything, now was the time. "It gets worse."

Beck lifted an eyebrow and waited for her to continue.

"He was a client and he fired me and my company when I told him about the baby."

A muscle jumped in Beck's jaw and his lips thinned. "Double douche."

"I promise you that sleeping with my clients is not what I do. He was the first guy since you and then there was you and I slept with you both. I've worked for you both!" She covered her face with her hands. "God, it's just so not me! I'm not the girl who does this!"

Beck pulled her hands from her face and rested his forehead on hers. "Did you know he was married? Did you sleep with him to get the contract?"

Cady slapped his shoulder. "No!"

"Then you didn't do anything wrong, Cades. With him or with me. So just let it go." Beck gripped the back of her neck and used his thumb to push her chin up. "You need to see a doctor and make sure everything is okay with the baby."

Cady grabbed the sheet and twisted it in her hand. "I'm scared, Beck. My mother miscarried a few times between Will and me, and Will was autistic. I'm scared they're going to find something wrong with the baby and—"

She hadn't really realized that was the way she felt until the words flew out of her mouth. She was scared and so very tired of being alone.

"I'll go with you, Cades."

"You don't have to," she said, not realizing that she'd wanted him with her. But now that he'd offered, she was desperately hoping that he would.

"I'll get Amy to find a decent OB-GYN and she'll make an appointment for you."

"Not this week. I'm crazy busy trying to finish the arrangements for the cocktail party and the exhibition and I have an industry awards dinner on Friday night. I don't suppose you'd—" No, of course he wouldn't be interested in accompanying her to one of the most boring functions on Planet Earth.

Beck smiled. "Are you asking me to come with you? As your date?"

"Yeah, sort of."

Beck kissed her once, his smile against her mouth. "Then I accept. And if we can get you a doctor's appointment, you're taking it, busy or not. But right now I want you naked and begging."

"You'll be late for your breakfast meeting," Cady breathlessly said, her hands skimming across his shoulders, down his hard pecs.

"They can wait."

Beck stared into her eyes, his mouth a breath away from hers, and he saw it on her face—desire—right before he kissed her.

At the first touch of his lips, she opened up and let him in. She ran her splayed hands against him, trying to make as much contact as possible with his hot, masculine skin.

His mouth snacked on hers, suckled and teased and she followed his lead, thinking that there was redemption and forgiveness in his kiss. His mouth on hers assured her that she was okay, that she was redeemable, that she was allowed to be imperfect and make mistakes.

Beck's hands moved under her T-shirt and pulled it up and over her head, dropping it to the floor. Then they slid up her sides, his thumbs brushing the undersides of her breasts. Cady murmured insensible words of encouragement, silently demanding him to touch her. His thumbs finally brushed her nipples as he dropped hot, openmouthed kisses along her jaw.

"More, more, more," Cady chanted.

"Not yet," Beck growled. "I want to see you, every beautiful inch of you."

He stood up, yanked away the covers and, with little ceremony, grabbed her ankles and pulled her so that she lay flat on her back, her legs slightly spread. She felt shy and exposed and her hand came up to shield her groin. Beck picked up her hand and lifted her knuckles to his lips. "Don't be shy, Cades. Not with me."

"I'm not nineteen, Beck. I'm pregnant, and my boobs are bigger."

His smile touched her fingers. "Bigger boobs are never a problem."

Cady jerked her fingers away. "Beckett! I'm being serious here."

"So am I." His hot, dark glance moved down her body, lingered on her breasts and then her crotch, and heated the skin on her tummy and thighs before returning to her face. "You're exquisite and I can't wait to touch you, taste you. Every inch of you."

Cady knew that he was struggling to keep himself from reaching for her, flabbergasted by the heat and passion in his deep, dark eyes. Under his hot gaze her inhibitions disappeared and she lifted her hand to touch her nipple, sliding her fingers down her abdomen to flirt with the small strip of hair at her thighs. "I'd much rather have you touch me and me touch you," she murmured.

"Oh, we'll get to that," Beck assured her.

Yet he still looked at her, seemingly content to enjoy the view. Frustrated with his lack of action,

Cady kneeled on the bed, dug her fingers between the towel and his six-pack and tugged his towel away. His erection jutted out from his groin, fantastically hard. Cady ran the tip of her index finger up his length and smiled when his erection jumped and his eyes closed. "I think you're beautiful, too, Beckett," she murmured.

She needed to taste him, to take him into her mouth, but she only managed a quick taste before Beck's strong arm banded around her stomach and he pulled her up his body. Her legs circled his hips and her ankles crossed just above his hard butt.

His penis probed her opening, hot and insistent, and Cady pushed down, feeling him slide inside her.

Cady smiled. He felt so amazing. "Love me, Beck." She pushed down, taking him inch by inch, and she groaned as he pushed his way into her, filling her.

Nothing felt as good as Beck loving her. Wanting more, wanting *everything*, she placed her mouth on his and lost herself in his kiss. It was kissing with no start or end point. Sure, sexy strokes of his tongue that echoed the action below.

Cady felt herself climbing, losing track of the here and now and what was real and not. Beck took her into another dimension where only they existed, two bodies intent to give pleasure. It was a battle of the best kind, both determined to give not receive, knowing that their lack of selfishness would result in their pleasure being redoubled.

Beck used his height, power and muscles to pick

her up and he walked her to the wall next to his bed. Cady felt the cool wall on her naked back, a perfect contrast to the hot man pressed to her front. Anchored to the wall, he allowed his hands to roam free and his hand trailed lightning down her back, over her hip, across her stomach. His hand moved up to cover her breast and he rubbed the center of his palm across her nipple then pulled it into a harder peak before dropping his head and laving it with his tongue.

He wanted all of her, she realized. He wanted her mindless with passion, feeling him on every inch of her skin. She did and Cady let out a deep, demanding moan, grinding down on him to take him farther into her, if that was at all possible. She wrenched her mouth off his. "Now! Dammit, Beck, now!"

Beck responded by slamming into her, pinning her to the wall, and when his hand pushed between their bodies to find her, she screamed and splintered into a million shards of pure orgasmic pleasure.

His entire body stilled and she clenched her inner muscles once, then twice, and her big man, so in control, lost it and followed her into oblivion.

Perfection, Cady thought, her forehead on his shoulder.

He was her first and, she thought, her last. He was the place she always, and only, wanted to be.

Feeling like this terrified her, the thought of walking away lifted the hair on her neck and arms.

Staying with him petrified her the most.

Ten

Feeling like he was about to jump out of his skin, Beck paced the small waiting room outside the technician's office and pushed his sleeve back to look at his watch. Dr. Bent was an OB-GYN and a friend of Amy and Julia's. She'd agreed to see Cady after her last patient of the day. Beck appreciated it but wished she'd hurry up. He wanted to get out of here, and fast.

Beck glanced at Cady, paging through a magazine on her lap. He'd left work to accompany her to this appointment, mostly because she might, accidentally-on-purpose forget the appointment. Her fears that there could be something wrong with this child weren't unfounded but being an ostrich wouldn't help her or the baby.

It was better, Beck thought, to face life head-on and deal with whatever problems arose. Yeah, maybe he had bullied Cady into seeing Dr. Bent but he needed to know that she was okay, that everything was as it should be.

He had a million things to do and a thousand fires to extinguish but Beck was rapidly coming to the conclusion that he'd do anything and be anywhere for Cady. What he felt for her ten years ago was not a fluke. She was just the adult version of the girl he'd loved so long ago.

Taking care of Cady was just something he did, something that was. Like the air he breathed, it was just there.

That didn't necessarily translate into living happily-ever-after. Like their vacation a decade ago, living and sleeping together was something that wouldn't last. She was gun-shy, and a permanent arrangement wasn't part of his master plan.

Neither was standing in a waiting room with a pregnant woman!

"Will you please go back to the office, Beckett?" Cady demanded. "You're making me nervous."

"No, if I do that you might leave without seeing the doctor."

Cady lifted her chin. "That would be rude after all the effort Amy and Julia went to to get this appointment."

Beck narrowed his eyes at her. "But you'd do it if you thought you could get away with it."

Cady slapped her magazine shut and threw it onto

the table next to her. "This just makes it all very real."

"I thought you puking was pretty real. And not being able to button your pants this morning makes it pretty real," Beck said, sitting down next to her and covering her hand with his. "I'm sure everything will be fine, Cades."

"Autism can be hereditary, Beck."

Beck pushed the palm of his hand under hers to link their fingers. "But it's not something that you diagnose early, so why avoid a doctor's appointment?"

"How do you know that?" Cady demanded, pulling back to look at him.

"I did some reading." Beck didn't bother telling her that when she moved in, he realized that what he knew about pregnancy could fit on a pinhead. He didn't like feeling ignorant so he ordered some books.

Okay, he ordered a lot of books and read most of them. He was now convinced that having babies was not for the faint of heart.

A tiny Asian woman appeared in the doorway and sent them a bright smile. "Cady Collins? I'm Dr. Giselle Bent. Come on through. Let's see what's what."

Cady stood up and Beck noticed the tremors in her fingers, her suddenly white face. Dr. Bent turned her megawatt smile on him. "Beck Ballantyne, I've heard a lot about you."

Beck shook her hand and sent her a wry grin. "Do not believe anything Amy and Julia have said about me."

The doctor laughed and motioned them down the hall.

Cady stood up, wincing as she did so. "Are you okay? What's the matter?" he demanded, walking over to her and placing his hand on her back.

"She has a very full bladder," Dr. Bent casually said.

Beck frowned. "I hate to state the obvious but—"

"We see the baby better with a full bladder," Dr. Bent said, opening the door to a small dark room containing a bed and, what Beck presumed, was the ultrasound machine.

Dammit, he'd forgotten about the full bladder thing. Typical Cady, she fried his brains.

Beck hovered in the doorway but the doctor motioned him into the room and told him to stand on the other side of Cady. "I'm going to do a quick ultrasound, then we'll head back for an exam and some blood tests. Lie down, open your pants and pull your top up."

Beck kept his eyes on Cady as she lay on her back, her eyes wide in her face. She quickly readied herself, rolling up her top under her breasts so that her belly was exposed. He'd kissed that skin last night, swirled his tongue around her belly button, traced a path down to between her legs.

He'd made her scream and cry and beg him for more.

Cady met his eyes and she raised an eyebrow. When he returned her stare with a bold look, she blushed and looked away. He knew that she'd flashed back to his bedroom and the explosive sex they'd shared.

He wanted more of that, wanted more of her. But he was balancing on a precarious pile of rocks and they were going to skitter out from under him at any minute. He had to take control of this situation. If he could corral his emotions, stop these flights of fancy, that would be a very good start.

Dr. Bent squirted gel on Cady's stomach and Cady cried, "That's cold!"

"Sorry." Dr. Bent pressed a wand on her stomach, and a picture flashed up on the monitor.

"Here we go," Dr. Bent said. Using her free hand, she pointed to the kidney-bean shape on the screen and flashed Cady a grin. "There's your baby. See that constant flash? That's the baby's heartbeat. We like to see that."

Neither Beck nor Cady reacted to her joke; they were both staring hard at the screen. Beck flicked Cady a look and saw tears in her eyes. He felt a lump form in his throat and when Cady held out her hand for his, the lump hardened.

As Dr. Bent turned up the volume on the ultrasound machine, he heard the *boom, boom, gurgle, boom* of the baby's heartbeat and wondered how he could describe something so elemental, so incredible. He felt both humble and blown away, in awe and ridiculously overexcited. The baby's heartbeat told him that he was utterly real, growing and on his way.

In a perfect world, that little blob should be his baby. Cady would be permanently his, rather than a temporary fling, the fiancée the world thought she might be. In a perfect world his parents wouldn't be dead, and he'd have another sibling. His parents would be playing with and spoiling their grandchildren.

Feeling this connected, this overwhelmed, this emotional, caused his throat to tighten and his heart to bang against his chest. Sweat pooled at the base of his spine and he felt disconnected from his body, like some unknown entity had its hands around his throat and he was battling to breathe. Panic attack, he realized.

He hadn't had one since standing in that crowded airport in Bangkok, watching Cady walk out of his life. Before that, he'd had a couple and usually handled them by diving into his training or into his books. Anything that was a distraction. As he grew up, they disappeared entirely.

It didn't escape his attention that Cady seemed to trigger these attacks, that she overwhelmed him, made him feel out of control. He swallowed, fighting his tight throat. He couldn't do that, couldn't go back to feeling so off balance. Being in control comforted him, made him feel like he could cope with the world and the demands it made on him. If he kept his life tightly controlled then he'd never feel like he was spinning off into an unknown and terrifying place.

He couldn't do this... He'd worked too damn hard to find this place where he didn't feel like fear was constantly nipping at his heels.

Cady terrified him. The attachment he felt to her,

and to that half-formed blob on the screen, scared the crap out of him. He was fit, wealthy and successful but this woman had the ability, with one look, word or touch, to cut him off at the knees.

Beck held up his hand, stepped back from the bed and shook his head. He had to get out of here…

Now.

There had only been one woman for him and she was it. But, like ten years ago, he couldn't take a chance on her, couldn't allow himself to be happy.

Cady looked from the screen to him and raised her eyebrows. "You're looking a bit pale. Are you okay?"

"Fine." Beck pushed the word out through gritted teeth. It was the biggest lie he'd ever uttered. "I just need some air."

Cady nodded and he saw her face tighten, her eyes dull. "I'm going to be a while, so why don't you head back to work. I'll see you back at your apartment."

Beck started to walk toward the door but then he stopped and looked back at the screen. He couldn't do it. Beck just stared at his lover, her eyes on the monitor, his mouth half open. Yes, he was scared and yes, he wanted to run, but if he quit this, if he quit them, he'd regret it for the rest of his life. He was terrified, and he felt like his heart was on a rope swing in his chest, but if he walked away from Cady for the second time, he wouldn't get another chance. Life only handed you a certain amount of opportunities to walk through the door. If you didn't, the door would eventually be permanently sealed.

Beck was self-aware enough to know what he was

doing: he was scared spitless and he was pushing her away. His first instinct when someone got close to him was to run them off but he'd wanted Cady enough that he'd allowed her to come closer than most. She'd sliced right through his emotional armor, and his internal alarm bells were ringing loudly. Habit screamed that he should retreat, that he should return to that place of safety where he needed no one and cared little for much beyond work and the occasional date.

He wasn't going to do it. He couldn't do it.

Beck walked back and placed his palms on the bed, staring hard at the screen. He wanted that baby to be his—oh, it was an irritation that the genes it carried weren't his but he believed in nurture versus nature. A passing on of DNA made a man a father, but time and effort made him a dad. He wanted to be there for Cady, be there for her child who would become his. He'd be there for his family, every step of the way.

He loved the baby's mother to distraction and he'd love her child as if it were his own. He wanted to take on the responsibility, and joy, of loving her and her child, and he wanted to be loved in return.

Maybe he didn't deserve love and a family. Maybe it was wrong for him to be happy. But he wasn't going to let those thoughts stop him from grabbing this chance to be with Cady. He wasn't going to miss out on another chance to have a family with her. Because they were meant to be together.

Whether he deserved it or not.

"Beck."

He jerked his head up and looked at Cady. Her face held no expression and he could see that she was biting the inside of her lip, a sure sign that she was nervous or worried. He reached out for her hand and when she jerked it away to avoid the contact, he frowned. What was that about?

"Go now, Beck," Cady said. Her voice was low but he heard the plea.

"Why?"

Her chest rose and fell and she looked to the monitor, her attention captured by the images there.

"I just need to be alone. Just me and my baby."

Now she wanted to be alone? What was that about? Beck, feeling hurt, looked at the doctor, who was pretending not to listen to their conversation. "But…"

"Beck, please. Just go."

Okay, he didn't understand but he wasn't about to have a fight and cause a scene. Cady was emotional and stressed and he'd just reached a life-changing decision. Maybe a little time apart would be a good idea. He could get his bouncing heart and careening emotions under control. Later he would tell her how he felt and they could discuss where to go and how to get there. All he was sure of was that if he walked away he'd be leaving everything that made his life joyful behind.

Not happening. Not again.

"We'll talk later," Cady told him, her tone resolute.

Beck quietly closed the door behind him. Yeah, they'd talk. But he wouldn't walk.

* * *

Cady stood in front of the door to Beck's apartment and waved her hands in front of her face to dry her tears. She blinked rapidly and pressed her fist to her sternum, trying to ease the burn.

Find your courage and open that damn door, Collins!

She knew this day was coming and she'd tried to prepare for it. She'd told herself over and over that she was living a fairy tale, that this was not reality, that she and Beck would end.

But she didn't expect it to happen in front of her eyes in a small dark room five minutes after looking at the blurry images of her baby.

She'd seen his retreat in his eyes, had read his thoughts as clearly as if he'd spoken his goodbyes. He couldn't cope with the emotion that was bubbling between them, their fierce attraction. With a baby on the way, she was just too much to cope with. Beck was overwhelmed and he was doing what he did best: distancing himself. She knew what would happen when she walked through this door. He would push her away.

The best predictor of future behavior is past behavior, Cady reminded herself. She wasn't going to let the past happen to her again. She'd walk away before he could toss her away again.

Still, the little girl inside her, the one so desperate to be loved, wanted him to make the grand gesture, to verbalize the words she most needed to hear.

I love you.

I will always love you.

I will always be at your side.

But Beck valued his freedom and his lone-wolf status more than he valued her, and she couldn't change that. Neither could she alter the fact that the people she most needed love and support from were the ones who were destined to disappoint her. It was better, easier and safer to walk this road by herself. She had her business and she had her baby. It would be enough. It had to be enough.

Cady felt a touch on her shoulder and then Beck was standing next to her, in front of the door. She'd been so lost in thought she hadn't heard him walk up to her. Cady straightened as he unlocked the door.

"Let's go inside," he said.

Cady walked into his apartment and headed straight for the stairs. Words, at this point, were superfluous so she headed for the master bedroom focused on what she needed to do next—pack her clothes that had accumulated over the past week. She remembered a suitcase in Beck's closet, tucked behind his shoes. She hauled it out and swung it onto the huge bed, where they'd loved and laughed, held each other through the night.

Beck appeared in the doorway to the room, his arms folded across his chest. "What are you doing?" he demanded.

"Packing."

Cady walked to the closet and grabbed the clothes he'd handed over to his cleaning service to take care of. She tossed them into the suitcase.

"Why?"

"Because this isn't working. You know it and I know it," Cady retorted.

"I thought it was," Beck replied, his words slow.

"Oh, come on, Beck. I know you have doubts about us. You always have! And we agreed that this was temporary."

Beck pushed an agitated hand through his hair. "It's natural to have doubts, Cady. It's a part of being in a relationship."

"We're not in a relationship! We're having a fling and I'm pregnant with another man's child."

His jaw tensed. "I consider that baby yours, not his. And, as I've said before, I don't have a problem with you being pregnant."

Cady snorted her disbelief. "That's just because you're getting fabulous sex."

Cady winced as hurt flashed across Beck's face. "That's not fair."

God, he sounded so calm. How could he stay so calm?

Cady returned to the closet and, fighting tears, picked up another pile of clothing. She threw it into the suitcase and stared down at the jumbled mess. "Please don't do this, Beck. Please don't give me hope that this can go anywhere."

"Maybe it can."

Cady shook her head. "I saw the doubts on your face before. You were this close." She held her thumb and forefinger slightly apart. "You were this close to bailing on me. You fought it this time, possibly because we're still really enjoying each other. But what happens when I'm fat and miserable and you decide that it's time to run? Will you stay or will you go? What happens when the urge to run becomes stronger than the urge to stay? I can't do that! I can't live like that. I can't—I won't—be tossed away again."

Beck walked over and held out his hand to her. Cady looked at it, fought the urge to jump into his arms and backed away. "I loved you once, Beck, with everything I had and you threw me away. It's not only me now. I have a child on the way. I can't risk you doing that to him."

"What can I say or do to get you to stay?"

"Nothing." She wiped away her tears. "Beck, what you can't handle, you walk away from."

"I'm standing here, trying not to!" Beck shouted. "I'm *trying*, Cady."

"Until the next time when you can't. You're a lone wolf, Beck. You're comfortable in that space. You've been that way since you were a child and that's your default mode of operation. When we hit a tight spot, you back away. That's what you did today."

"Yet I am still here, asking you to stay."

"Today was supposed to be a happy day, Beck. We saw a new life, it was fantastic and you got scared. What happens when something else rocks us? How will you react then? Can I rely on you to be there? Would we stand together and deal with it or would you go off on your own?"

"We'd stand together." He said the right words but

she couldn't believe him. If she believed him and she was wrong, she'd pay too big a price.

"You say that but that's not what you do. You dealt with your parents' deaths on your own and you kept the secret of your mom being pregnant from your siblings. That's you staying in your space, dealing with crap on your own."

Beck blanched and Cady fought the urge to touch him, to say to hell with it and take the chance. But it wasn't wise and it damn well wasn't smart. "Somebody very wise once said, 'There's nothing worse than being lonely with the person you love.' I'd rather be lonely on my own, Beck."

Cady zipped her suitcase, not sure if she had everything but knowing that she needed to leave while she still could. Before Beck talked her into staying.

She lifted the suitcase off the bed and placed it on its wheels.

"What about the campaign, your contract?" Beck asked, his voice and face tight.

"We're professionals, remember? We can communicate via email." Cady sighed and rubbed her forehead with her hand. "From a business point of view, we're in a good place. We never admitted to being engaged, so if we stop seeing each other, the attention will fade without any major repercussions. Sage's new line is a massive success and the ads are making an impact. After the exhibition and cocktail party, where Sage will reveal even more new designs, I have no doubt you'll capture that new, young, rich market you're after. It's all good, Beck."

"But you're still walking."

"I'm still walking."

"Don't go, Cady."

She looked at him. God, she was going to miss him. "I have to. We have the ability to rip each other apart. I survived that once. I won't again. The stakes are too high, Beck."

"If we close this door, it stays closed, Cady."

Cady forced her feet to walk over to him. She stood on her toes to drop a kiss on his cheek. "I love you, Beck, but my love isn't enough. I need to know that you'll stick. But sticking isn't what you do."

Eleven

Cady rested her hand on her abdomen as she heard the click of her mother's low heels on the wooden floor on the other side of her door. This wasn't going to be a pleasant conversation but she was tired of lying—to herself and to her parents. Last night, with Beck, was the first time in years that she'd been completely authentic with the people she loved.

He'd just stared at her, shocked, and let her leave. Underneath all the sadness, in the odd spaces that weren't totally devastated, she felt…cleaner. There was a freedom in truth, in being honest, in dealing with what was, not what you wanted it to be.

The front door opened and Cady caught her mother's surprise before her how-nice-to-see-you expression crossed her face. Edna leaned forward so that Cady could drop the briefest kiss on her cheek and stepped back into the house. "I wasn't expecting you."

Cady heard the undertone of "how rude of you not to call" and stepped into her childhood home. She shouldn't need to call, shouldn't have to give her parents advance warning of her visit. Her child would be raised knowing that there was a key to their house under the mat, that there was food in the fridge, a warm bed in the spare room. Her home would always be her child's home, his refuge, his soft place to fall.

"Your father is in his study. Let me call him," Edna said, her fingers playing with her fake-pearl necklace. It was late afternoon but her mom's makeup was perfect, her white blouse spotless.

She was so concerned with looking the part, she never lived.

"Why don't we take this chat to Dad's study, Mom?" Cady suggested, dropping her leather bag on the hall table. She smiled when her mom picked her bag up and hung it over a hook behind the door.

Edna waved at the formal room just off the hallway. "But we always meet our guests here."

"But I'm not a guest, Mom, I'm your daughter," Cady stated as she walked down the hall toward her father's study. At the door, she hesitated, thinking that she could count the times on one hand that she'd entered this hallowed sanctum. There was no way that her father and mother had made love on his desk the way she and Beck had in his office the other night. It had been fun and hot and raunchy and exciting...

Beck. Dammit. Tears welled and her stomach knotted and she wanted to sink to the floor. Instead, she hauled in a breath and ordered herself not to think about him. She'd cry later, when she was alone.

She knocked once and turned the handle on the door. "Hey, Dad, I'm invading your man cave!"

Bill Collins looked up at her over the tops of his glasses. He sent Edna a quick look and raised his eyebrows. "Were we expecting you, Cady?" he asked in his formal voice.

Cady walked over to the corner of his desk, moved a couple of books and hopped up onto the desk, her feet dangling. "You see, Dad, that's part of what I wanted to talk to you about. Why do you need advanced warning? Shouldn't you be happy to see me?"

Edna exchanged a long look with her husband before walking up to Cady and lightly resting her fingers on Cady's shoulder. "What's this about, Cady Rebecca?"

"It's about your expectations of me." Cady jumped down from the desk and walked to the bay window, pulling the drape aside to look at her mom's now barren garden. A light dusting of snow covered the paving stones and the angel statues and the roof of the birdhouse.

"Beck and I broke up," Cady said, stating the fact without emotion and waited for them to detonate. When her statement was met with silence, she turned around and threw up her hands. "Oh, right, you didn't know that Beck and I have been seeing each other again."

"Why didn't you tell us?" Bill asked.

"I thought you'd freak," Cady admitted.

"I'm sorry that it's over and I'm sorry you didn't tell us," Bill said, placing his elbows on his desk, his eyes steady on her face. "I know that you love him very much and that it must hurt."

"It does." Cady frowned. "Why do you think I love him?"

"Cady, you always have." Edna perched on one of the leather chairs and linked her hands. "From the first moment you saw him, I knew he was going to break your heart."

Cady shrugged. "It wasn't for the first time."

Edna nodded. "We suspected that's what happened after you returned from Thailand."

Cady pushed her hands into the kangaroo pockets of her sweatshirt. "That wasn't the first time my heart broke, Mom. It broke the day you sent Will away, and it broke again when he died. It broke a little every time you told me I couldn't play with a Barbie doll or look at a fashion magazine or watch a program on TV."

Cady heard her parents' swift intake of breath but trying to hold back her words was like trying to use a cork to hold back a flood. "When you try to fix something that's not broken, you end up breaking it. In your quest for a perfect child, by sending a perfect child away from his home, without explaining why, you broke...me."

"Jesus God."

It wasn't a blasphemy, more like a desperate plea from her father's mouth to God. Cady saw the horror on their faces and she felt a quick spurt of sympathy. They were like two balloons, full of hot air, and she'd just jammed a red-hot poker into them. She didn't want to hurt them but she also realized that, until she stood up for herself, she couldn't stand up for the child growing inside her, the child she would be raising alone.

"I didn't come here to criticize you but to explain a few things." She looked at her dad. "Congratulations on the promotion to the big church, Dad, but maybe you should tell them that your daughter is going to be a single mom raising a married man's child."

"Beck is married?" Bill shouted.

"No, of course not. Beck isn't the father. I was in a relationship with a guy who I thought was divorced but he wasn't."

"Cady!"

Cady whipped around and met her mother's shocked eyes. "Yeah, Mom, I know, I messed up. But you know what? Real people mess up! They wear jeans and get bad marks at school and run away with their boyfriends to Thailand! They get pregnant and they fall in love and get their hearts broken." Cady felt the hot slide of tears down her face. "I just wanted to tell you the truth. I'm tired of lying and I am so tired of trying to be the pastor's perfect kid. I'm not a kid anymore and I'm not perfect. I'm just human."

Cady wiped the tears off her cheeks. Her parents looked shell-shocked and her mother was doing a fantastic impersonation of a goldfish. Her dad removed his glasses and tapped them against the desk.

"So, I'll go now. Next time I'll call." Cady pushed her hair back from her forehead as she walked to the open study door, the space behind her heavy and loaded with tension.

"We sent Will away because we thought he could hurt you."

Her father's words stopped her in her tracks. Not sure if she'd heard him correctly, she slowly turned. "What did you say?"

Bill stood up and folded his thin arms across his narrow chest. "His behavior took a turn for the worse when he hit puberty. For some reason he never acted up around you but when you were at school, he became impossible."

Cady felt anger bubble in her chest. "I don't believe you."

"Do you remember that day you came home from school and the fire department was here?" her mom asked.

"Yeah. You told me that you were ironing in Will's room and you left the iron on and somehow the room caught fire."

"Will found a lighter and set fire to the curtains. He also started punching me. The last straw was when he tried to stab me with a potato peeler," Edna said, her voice coated with pain. "You never saw it but he was starting to hurt you, too."

"He was not!" Cady protested, not quite able to believe what she was hearing.

"The hair-pulling, the playful pinches that made you cry?" her mom shot back. "He was getting so much bigger, stronger. I couldn't control him or his rages. Dammit, why do you insist on seeing me as the bad guy, Cady?"

"He was uncontrollable, Cady," her father said, "and we thought a residential home was best for him. And you." He looked at her and she saw the truth in his eyes.

Oh, God. Her parents were right. If she pulled the rose-colored glasses off and looked at the past clearly, she could see how her brother had changed, had become meaner and bigger.

"You were trying to protect me?"

Bill nodded and Cady pushed her hair back from her face in sheer frustration. "Why the hell didn't you talk to me? I thought that if I colored outside of the lines I'd be sent away, too."

"Oh, God," Bill muttered.

"Seriously, for a pastor and a pastor's wife, you both suck at communication!" Cady cried.

Bill walked over to her and gently, hesitantly wrapped his arms around her. It was the first hug she'd had from her father in too many years to count. "I'm so sorry."

"Me, too." Cady laid her head on his chest. "I'm

sorry if my being single and pregnant causes you trouble in your new job."

"Screw them."

Cady let out a strangled laugh and tightened her arms around her father. He gave her an awkward pat on her back and led her out the door. "Now, my girl, you and your mom and I are going to have a chat. A real, no-holds-barred, soul-deep conversation."

"I don't need a preacher, Dad, and I don't need counseling."

"Maybe you don't," her father agreed. "Maybe you just need to talk to your mom and dad."

Sitting on the edge of his sofa, Beck watched as his siblings walked across the laminate floor toward him, their faces somber. Sage sat down beside him and wrapped her arm around his bicep, her head on his shoulder. Linc headed to the kitchen, grabbed a bottle of wine from his enormous wine rack and handed it to Jaeger to open. He pulled four wine-glasses down from the cupboard and returned to the living area.

His brothers sat, wine was poured and sipped, and no one spoke.

They were all waiting for him to start. After all, he'd summoned them here.

Beck loosened the tie strangling him and encountered his burning skin beneath his open collar. Still no air. So he couldn't blame the tie for his constricted throat.

God, how was he going to do this? He had to, he

knew that, but how? He wished Cady was here, sitting next to him, his hand on her thigh, encouragement in her eyes. Beck ran his hand over his face, trying to push away the image of her stricken expression, her eyes reflecting her soul-deep pain.

She'd walked away and he now knew how it felt. But it was the right thing to do, Beck assured himself. Because he knew it couldn't last; nothing that wonderful did. The connection they shared was magic, a mirage, an illusion. It wasn't real.

It couldn't be. And, because he'd started to believe in those concepts, to fall in love with being in love, with the normality of having a partner and child on the way, they'd hurt each other. Again.

"You're starting to scare us, Beck," Jaeger said, his voice low but concerned.

Sage squeezed his arm. "Are you sick?" she demanded. "Whatever is wrong, we'll get you the best medical help, fly you wherever you need to go."

Beck briefly touched her knee. "I'm not sick, Sage. Not physically, anyway." Beck made himself look at Jaeger. "I'm sorry that I asked you to come alone, to leave Piper at home, but I just wanted the four of us here. The siblings."

Jaeger nodded his understanding.

Beck hauled in a sharp breath and looked at Linc. "What I have to say was before your time but you're our brother, so here you are."

Linc mirrored Beck's body language and rested his forearms on his knees, holding his wineglass in a loose grip between them. "And you're our brother and whatever the hell this is about, we stand by you."

He'd see if that held true after he'd told them what he had to say. He knew he had to release the truth; he couldn't keep this secret anymore. It was too heavy to carry anymore. Cady was right about that.

Beck sat up straight and looked at each of his siblings. "Our parents were killed in that plane crash because I asked them to come home to be with me because I was having that operation to put a pin in my wrist."

Their expressions didn't change from wary expectation, so Beck plowed on. "What you don't know is that Mom was four months pregnant when they died. She was expecting another child. We would've had another sibling."

Beck waited for the shocked surprise, the hot outrage. Linc looked sympathetic, Jaeger thoughtful, and Sage's eyes filled with tears.

"Oh, man, that's horrible," she said. "Poor Mom and Dad. Poor little baby."

Jaeger stared into his wineglass for a long time before lifting his head and pinning Beck to his seat with his penetrating eyes. "How do you know this, Beck?"

"After the funeral, I was hiding under a table in the living room. Do you remember Dr. Blaine?"

Jaeger frowned. "Vaguely."

"Maybe I knew him better because he treated me for my arm. He was also Mom's doctor and I heard him talking to his wife—his nurse—about Mom's pregnancy."

"God, Beck." Through his cotton shirt Beck felt Sage's lips touch his shoulder. "Why didn't you tell us?"

Beck shrugged. He stood up abruptly and walked over to the closest window, keeping his back to his siblings.

"Beck!" His name was like a bullet on Jaeger's lips. "Why didn't you tell us?"

He couldn't answer that, not without cutting his heart open and allowing all his fears and guilt to gush to the floor.

"Because he thought you'd blame him for that, too," Linc said in his calm, measured voice.

"What the hell do you mean by that?" Jaeger demanded. "We've never blamed him for anything!"

Beck turned slightly to look at Linc, his brother through choice and not blood, and tried to push the ball of emotion down his throat. Linc understood, he realized. He'd understood far more than Beck gave him credit for.

"Tell them, Beck," Linc said. "You need to."

Beck turned and pushed his hands into the pockets of his suit pants, rocking on his heels. *Now or never, Beck. Just spill it and get it done.*

"I've always felt guilty for our parents' deaths and I blamed myself. I've always thought that you might blame me, too, just a little bit."

"But why?" Sage cried. "Why would you think that?"

"Because I asked them to come home! I was the whiny, needy kid who needed his mommy to hold his hand when he went into the hospital. I was the reason their plane flew into a freakin' mountain, killing them and the baby!"

Silence, pure and saturated with emotion, filled the space between them.

"Are you friggin' nuts?" Jaeger finally roared as he jumped up and stormed over to him.

Beck braced for a punch but Jaeger just gripped his neck in his hand and pulled his head down so that their foreheads touched and their eyes were level.

"You did not do this," Jaeger stated. "This was not your fault."

"But—"

"Not your fault," Jaeger reiterated, his eyes boring into his. "Jesus, Beck! How could you think that I would blame you for that? You were a kid!"

"I never blamed you, either."

Beck pulled his head away from Jaeger to look at Sage, who was in Linc's arms, tears running down her face. "Really?"

"You lost them, too, Beck. We all did," Sage said, between sobs.

"But the baby—"

"It happened, bro." Jaeger dropped his hand and stepped back, his eyes suspiciously bright. "Yeah, it's sad and yeah, we've missed them, but why you would take this on yourself, I have no damn idea."

"Why don't we have some wine and talk about that?" Linc suggested. He sat down in the chair and

Sage, like she'd done when she was little, sat on his lap, her arms looped around his neck. Beck felt the slap of a memory: Sage sitting in Linc's arms, him sitting at his feet, Jaeger standing behind them, a unit, a team. Them against the world.

He bit his lip, desperate to keep the tears from sliding down his face. He'd done them a disservice not talking to them about this, not talking to them about the wounds that hadn't really healed.

"I called them home. It was my fault they ran into bad weather," Beck said, picking up a glass of wine from the table and taking a fortifying breath.

Jaeger lifted his hand. "Stop! Dad was reckless. We know that. He took chances. He should not have flown if there was a chance of the weather turning."

Point taken, Beck thought, feeling the pressure start to ease off his chest.

"It was their job to be with you, Beck," Linc said. "It's what parents do. Your kid calls and no matter what you're doing, you run. I'd do that for Shaw. Jaeger and Piper would do that for Ty."

"Do you get that?" Jaeger demanded.

"It's starting to sink in," Beck admitted.

"Keep going, Beck. Get it all out," Linc ordered.

He didn't want to but he knew that this was an emotional abscess that needed to be lanced. And he was halfway there…

"Because I felt guilty, I thought I had to prove my worth to you, to this family. I had to show you I was worth loving." Beck felt like every word was being dragged up his throat.

"So that explains your constant studying, constant training. God, you were a pain in the ass," Jaeger commented, a hint of amusement on his face. He looked at Linc. "It was hell standing in the shadow of our younger brother."

"It really was. Then you grew taller and bigger and we really started to hate you," Linc agreed and Beck saw the mischief in his eyes.

Sage ignored their teasing and climbed off Linc's lap to walk to him. She took his hand. "Connor worried about you, more than he worried about the rest of us." She tossed a saucy look at her two older brothers before continuing. "Connor said that God would protect the stupid, so he didn't worry that much about Dumb and Dumber over there. But he worried about you. I think he knew that you blamed yourself."

Linc nodded. "He was always telling you to go easy, to not work so hard, give so much. That you were perfectly okay, being who you were."

"That's why he made you travel after college," Sage added. "Why he insisted you take a break every few months. It was his way of protecting you from burnout. You give too much of yourself to work, too little of yourself to life. And love."

Beck met Sage's vivid blue eyes and realized that she knew that he and Cady were over. He saw her frustration. "You shouldn't have pushed her away, Beck. She's the only one who's ever really got you."

"She left me this time," Beck replied.

"She left before she could be hurt again," Sage

told him, her eyes worried. "She loves you, Beck. Anyone can see that."

"I don't—"

"I swear to God, if you say that you don't deserve her, I'll punch you!" Jaeger shouted. "You don't find love twice and push it away, you moron! You fight for it, you hold on to it, you do everything you can to keep it." Jaeger threw up his hands in disgust. "You're the smart one, so why am I spelling this out for you?"

Sage rolled her eyes at him and then Linc. "Was this the same brother who nearly lost his fiancée and son because he was being a moron? Or was that Jaeger's alter ego?"

"I think it was the other Jaeger," Linc murmured.

"Smart asses," Jaeger growled. "The point is—"

"I know what the point is," Beck said. And he did. The point was Cady. The point was that he loved her and wanted her in his life. He always had, always would.

"He's seeing the light…thank God and all his angels and archangels," Jaeger stated, sarcastically.

"I have to find her right now," Beck said. "I have to talk to her."

"That would be a very good idea," Sage said, smiling.

Beck patted the front pockets of his pants and then the back pockets. "I need my car keys. And my car. Where are my keys? My phone?"

Jaeger picked up his keys from the glass bowl on the counter and threw them at Beck. Beck snatched them out of thin air and picked up his phone from the coffee table. "Okay. I can go." He jerked his head up and looked at Sage. "What do I say?"

"Keep it simple, stupid. Say you're sorry for being a moron man, that you are a moron man and ask her to forgive you."

Beck frowned at her. That advice sounded a tad snarky. Like she had an ax to grind with his gender. But he couldn't think about that now.

"Right. Brooklyn. I've got to go to Brooklyn. Crap. That's going to take me forever." Beck moaned, now desperate to get to Cady, to be with Cady, to start his life. Then he remembered something else he needed to take and he ran into the kitchen and started yanking open drawers, sure what he needed was in one of them. He tossed random junk onto the floor and let out a victorious yell when his hand found what he was looking for. He shoved the item into his back pocket and looked around.

"This can work. I can do this," he muttered.

"He's looking a little green and a lot unhinged," Jaeger commentated, now openly amused.

"God help him when Cady goes into labor," Linc commented. "He's going to be a friggin' basket case. Get a grip, Beckett."

"Right." Beck pulled in what he hoped was a calming breath. "Cady, Brooklyn, ask for another chance."

"Oh, wait...she's not in Brooklyn," Sage told him. "She's in Chelsea, at that awards dinner you promised to accompany her to before you broke her heart."

Beckett looked at his watch, noticed the date and remembered that it was Friday. Also known as Day Four of Hell On Earth. It was also the date scheduled for the PR industry awards.

"Practice your groveling, dude," Jaeger suggested. "You're going to need it."

"You should know," Linc murmured and ignored the subtle middle finger Jaeger showed him but hid from Sage.

"Okay, let's go." Beck went to his door, held it open and gestured for them to leave.

Linc lifted his glass up to the light and swirled the red liquid around. "Fat chance. We're going to stay here and drink your wine."

Fair, Beck decided.

Twelve

Cady felt like the single girl at a wedding. Sitting alone at the table, she glared at the untouched place setting beside her. Two weeks ago she thought that she'd have a partner for this event, but looking from the crowded dance floor to the people milling at the bar, she was the only person in the room without a date.

How sad.

But even sitting here alone was better than returning to her empty, small apartment, to her cold, small bed. She hadn't been able to sleep in her bed since she left Beck's loft a few days ago, and the little sleep she'd managed was curled up in her chair by the window.

Cady rolled her head, trying to work out the knots her unorthodox sleeping position caused. She missed lying on Beck's chest, craved his big arms around her, missed rubbing her silky legs against his muscular limbs. She missed his deep breathing, his propensity to hog the covers...

She missed Beck sliding into her, emotionally and physically, filling up those deep, secret places nobody else could reach.

Cady stared at her glass of water, blinking away the tears in her eyes. Would this pain ever go away? She'd thought she'd experienced heartbreak when she was younger, but this, like their passion, bit deeper, burned brighter. This time around, the pain squeezed and pummeled, was a concentrated ball of agony. Cady felt Beck had whittled a hole into her soul and that it was irreparable.

It was something she suspected she'd have to live with the rest of her life.

Despite how much she loved him, she'd made the right decision to leave while she could. While she felt like half a person, she knew that this pain was better than hanging around, waiting for the day when Beck had had enough, when he ran out again. Living with that indecision would eat away at her, would slowly erode her soul.

A cracked, battered soul was better than none at all.

Her phone buzzed and she smiled when she saw the message from her mom.

I hope you're taking your vitamins and are getting enough sleep. Love you.

Her mother was trying and Cady couldn't fault her for that. She didn't know whether they would ever have a true mother-daughter relationship but she hoped so. She knew now that there were some things you couldn't force. Her parents were her parents. And Beck was Beck. She couldn't force any of them to give her what she needed.

Cady picked up her clutch from the table and pushed her chair back. There was no point in staying here any longer. She would go home, climb into her chair and finish the rest of that carton of chocolate ice cream. Yeah, she was going to get fat but so what? She was pregnant and eating for two.

Okay, she was also overdosing on ice cream because she was miserable but nobody needed to know that.

Cady was about to stand up when a broad hand appeared in front of her, holding a tube of glue. She instantly recognized that hand, those fingers that loved her so well, the strong wrist and forearm, the cuffs and sleeves of his button-down shirt rolled back to reveal sculpted muscles.

Cady couldn't look up so she looked down, her eyes flying over his flat stomach and down his long legs, still wearing black suit pants.

She watched, astounded, as Beck hooked a chair with his foot and dragged it closer to her and then he was in her space, taking up her air. She lifted her gaze to his face, noticing his red eyes and heavily bearded jaw.

Beck took her clenched fist resting on her knee

and gently pried her fingers open. When her palm was open he put the tube of glue in her hand.

Cady frowned, puzzled. "Glue?"

Beck nodded. "Super glue. Strong as hell."

"I don't get it, Beck," she said, holding the tube out to him.

"I'll stick, Cades. I promise."

Her eyes bounced between his face and the tube of glue and the seconds ticked by.

"I'll stick, Cades." He repeated the words. "I might get scared and feel like I want to but I won't run, I promise."

Cady felt her heart starting to defrost. "What will you do if you don't run?"

Beck lifted a powerful shoulder. "Talk to you, take you to bed, kick my own ass and remind myself that you are the most important person in my life. I'll remind myself that I never want to feel the way I do now—lost, alone, a little crazy."

She wanted to believe him, she did, but she was terrified of reaching out and taking what she so desperately needed. "Why are you doing this, Beckett?"

His hands moved to the backs of her knees to capture her legs between his, to connect them together. "I love you, babe. I loved you in Thailand, I loved you while we were apart and I've loved you every second since we met again. It's always been you, Cady. Nobody else has ever made me feel the way you do."

Cady wanted to howl with joy but she forced that treacherous emotion away. Love wasn't enough…

"It is, Cady, if it's you and me," Beck said, and Cady realized that she'd spoken the words out loud. "But it's more than love between us. It's friendship, it's hope. It's trust. It's me believing that I deserve this, that I'm allowed to be happy, and it's you trusting me not to run and leave you behind. It's us—" he touched her tummy with the tips of his fingers "—raising this child and our other children with heart and humor, trying not to mess them up as we do. It's laughing together and loving together and living together."

Beck lifted his hand to cradle her face, his thumb rubbing her lower lip. "It's waking up and kissing this face for the rest of my life. It's your hand I want to hold, your body I want to love, your mind I want to explore." Beck's thumb glided over the wet skin beneath her eye. "Don't cry, Cades."

She didn't know that she was. Her heart was just so full of love it was leaking from her eyes. She curled her hand around his neck and fell into the love he was openly offering.

"Tell me that I can stick, Cady."

"God, yes," she murmured, touching her lips to his. "Stick to me, with me, by me, Beck."

He groaned, his lips tenderly tasting hers. "I love you so much. I always have."

"Me, too. Let's not do this again, okay?"

"Deal," Beck replied, pulling back. He looked around, looked down at his clothing and pulled a face. "You look like a million bucks. I love that dress and can't wait to get you out of it—but I think I'm slightly underdressed. I'm not even wearing a tie."

"I can't tell you how little I care," Cady told him, resting her hand on his knee.

Beck picked up her left hand to look at the bare ring finger on it. "This finger looks like it needs something on it."

"I like your mom's ring," Cady said, her voice breathless. She couldn't believe this was really happening.

"I do, too," Beck said, his voice full of emotion. "I'd give it to you if I could."

Cady rested her hand on his heart. His offer touched her deeply and if she had the slightest doubts about his staying power after his declaration earlier, they were now thoroughly banished.

"Ring or no ring, Beck, I'm yours. I always have been."

Beck held her face in his big hands, kissed her gently, reverently. "Then I am the luckiest guy in the world. I love you. Let's go home."

Cady allowed him to pull her to her feet, to tuck her into his side. Next to him, side by side, walking through life…this was what she was meant to do.

Cady placed a hand on his arm and Beck looked down at her, love in his eyes. When she couldn't push her words past the emotion clogging her throat, he squeezed her hand, silently encouraging her.

"Thank you for loving me, for loving my baby." Cady's voice broke on the words.

"That's so easy to do. It has always has been." Beck laid his hand on her rounded stomach. "Our baby, Cades. Our lives, our future, our children."

Cady nodded and felt the last vestiges of her tension drain away. How wonderful it was to feel like her life was clicking together instead of falling apart, she thought as she walked hand in hand with Beck toward her future. Their future, she corrected herself, on a huge internal smile.

She wasn't alone anymore. She'd never be alone again.

Epilogue

Cady looked around the exquisitely decorated ball-room, her eyes jumping from the bar to the security and from famous guest to famous guest. The gems were safe, tucked away in their pressure-sensitive, unable-to-be-shattered transparent boxes; the guests were behaving themselves and everyone loved Sage's new designs.

Ballantyne International was back, stronger than before. Talking about the Ballantynes, Cady looked across the room and smiled at the clan standing in the corner. Three brawny brothers looking rather yummy in their designer tuxes, and their black-haired, blue-eyed elf of a sister. Cady placed her hand on her stomach and felt tears prick her eyes.

They were her family now. Her baby would be

raised a Ballantyne. Maybe, Cady thought on an internal smile, all her clean living as a child was paying off.

Beck caught her gaze, gave her a slow smile that heated his eyes and the fabric of the minuscule thong she wore under her American-rose ball gown. Picking up the hem of her dress, she placed her fingers on top of the box holding Beck's mom's engagement ring and silently thanked her for the blessing of her son, promising her that she'd love him forever.

Cady quickly moved over to the Ballantynes and Beck held out his hand, pulling her into his side. They were joined by Tate, who looked fabulous in a vintage, boho-inspired ball gown. Judging by Linc's inability to keep his eyes off her, Linc thought so, too.

Standing with her back to Beck's chest, his arm across her stomach, Cady watched Sage, who was scowling at a sexy guy across the room. Cady immediately understood why Sage couldn't take her eyes off him. Nearly as tall as Beck, as broad-shouldered, he was a curious mix of Asian and European with dark, sultry eyes and a bright smile.

Cady watched, intrigued, as the man turned around, caught Sage's eyes across the room and gave her a look that said, "I know what's under that dress and I like it." He lifted his tumbler of amber liquid, took a sip and watched her over the rim of the glass.

Cady nudged Sage with her elbow. "Phew! That was hot. Like volcanic."

Sage broke their heated stare by giving him a kiss-my-ass look and when she turned her head, Cady saw the misery in Sage's eyes.

"Yeah, hot. And I got burned." Sage's shoulders rose and fell, and she turned her back on the guy to take both of Cady's hands in hers. "I am so happy that you and Beck are together. Welcome to the family, Cady." Sage briefly touched her rounded tummy. "And I can't wait to meet your and Beck's baby."

Their baby. Cady sighed and leaned into Beck. He was going to adopt her child and was going to raise him, or her, as his own. How lucky could she get?

"Thank you." Cady tossed a smile at Beck before looking back at Sage. "By the way, I thought you promised to pay me if I took another brother off your hands."

Sage laughed. "I did promise you that. And I always deliver. Jaeger has your payment." Sage tossed a mischievous look at Beck, who was now tuned in to their conversation. "And it's Cady's present, not yours, Beckett."

Beck stepped back but kept his hand, warm and loving, on Cady's hip. "What is?" he asked, puzzled.

Jaeger pulled a small white paper square out of the inside pocket of his tuxedo and tossed it at Beck. He snatched the packet out of the air and Cady watched excitement build in his eyes. "You got it?" he asked Jaeger, sounding like a kid on Christmas morning.

Jaeger looked seriously pleased with himself. "I did. I worked my ass off tracking it down and I did some very hard negotiating. Bribery and coercion might've been involved. You owe me, brother. Big-time."

Linc touched Beck's shoulder with his big hand and he smiled. "I'll send you the bill. I expect full payment right away."

Beck raised his eyebrows, laughter in his eyes. "No discount?"

"It's four carat, rare as hell and practically flaw-less," Linc retorted and then smiled. "Okay, five per-cent."

"Hey, I paid full price!" Jaeger complained, but everyone ignored him as they watched Beck open the small packet.

It's a Ballantyne thing, Cady told herself. She'd have to get used to the world stopping when the sibs found a rare and precious gem. She sent Tate a sym-pathetic smile as four heads obscured her view of whatever caught their interest.

Remembering that she was still there to work, Cady pulled the cuff up on Beck's wrist to look at his watch and thought that it was time for the dance floor to open. As she started to walk away, Beck grabbed her wrist to keep her at his side.

"Where do you think you are going?" he asked.

Cady gestured to the ballroom. "I have something to take care of."

Beck cast his eyes over the room. "Everything is fine. I thought you might like to look at what Jae-ger found."

Cady nodded, thinking that a couple of minutes couldn't hurt. But she couldn't forget that they were paying the musicians by the hour and she needed to check on—

At the sight of the pink-red stone, resting on the white paper, her throat slammed closed. Oh, God, that was a red beryl, luscious, deep, sexy. It was a little smaller than the stone in his mom's ring but just as beautiful. Cady placed her hand on her heart and looked up at Beck, biting her lip as she noticed the depth of love in his eyes.

For her, all for her.

"It's beautiful." Cady touched the stone with the tip of her finger.

"Yeah, it is." Beck picked up the stone and placed it in the palm of her hand. He opened the paper it was wrapped in and held it up for her to see the ring design on the paper, beautifully rendered. It was his mom's ring but a little more modern, a little edgier. This was Sage's beautiful work.

"For me?" Cady whispered.

"Yeah," Beck replied, his voice husky with emotion. "Sage will make it for us."

"It's beautiful," Cady said, feeling overwhelmed. She blinked away her tears, gripping Beck's forearm to keep her balance. "I would've been really happy to wear your mom's ring. That one, over there." She glanced to the glass case that housed the copy.

"No wife of mine is going to wear a fake ring," Beck told her. A small smile touched his lips. "You are going to be my wife, aren't you, Cades?"

She smiled and cradled his face. "I really am. And I love the ring. But I'll always love you more."

Beck leaned down to rest his forehead against hers and his smile heated her from the inside out. "Welcome to the rest of our lives, Cades."

"Two down, one to go," Sage stated, sounding pleased with herself. "I'm making progress."

*   *   *   *   *

*If you liked this story of billionaires in love,
pick up these other novels from Joss Wood:*

*TAKING THE BOSS TO BED
TRAPPED WITH THE MAVERICK MILLIONAIRE
PREGNANT BY THE MAVERICK MILLIONAIRE
MARRIED TO THE MAVERICK MILLIONAIRE
HIS EX'S WELL-KEPT SECRET*

Available now from Harlequin Desire!

*   *   *

*If you're on Twitter, tell us what you think of
Harlequin Desire! #harlequindesire*

Get 2 Free Books,
Plus 2 Free Gifts—

HARLEQUIN *Desire*

just for trying the Reader Service!

*After a fling with a sexy marine leaves Rita pregnant,
her attempts to reach the billionaire are met with
silence…until now! Brooding, reclusive Jack offers to
marry Rita—in name only. Will his new family give him
the heart to embrace life—and love—again?*

*Read on for a sneak peek of
LITTLE SECRETS: HIS UNEXPECTED HEIR
by USA TODAY bestselling author Maureen Child.*

Jack didn't make a habit of coming here. Memories were
thick and he tended to avoid them, because remembering
wouldn't get him a damn thing. But against his will, images
filled his mind.

Every damn moment of that time with Rita was etched
into his brain in living, vibrant color. He could hear the
sound of her voice. The music of her laughter. He saw the
shine in her eyes and felt the silk of her touch.

"And you've been working for months to forget it," he
reminded himself in a mutter. "No point in dredging it up
now."

What they'd found together all those months ago was
over. There was no going back. He'd made a promise to
himself. One he intended to keep.

It was a hard lesson to learn, but he had learned it in the
hot, dry sands of a distant country. And that lesson haunted
him to this day.

But Jack Buchanan didn't surrender to the dregs of fear, so he kept walking, made himself notice the everyday world pulsing around him. Along the street, a pair of musicians was playing for the crowd and the dollar bills tossed into an open guitar case. Shop owners had tables set up outside their storefronts to entice customers and, farther down the street, a line snaked from a bakery's doors all along the sidewalk.

He hadn't been downtown in months, so he'd never seen the bakery before. Apparently, though, it had quite the loyal customer base. Dozens of people—from teenagers to career men and women—waited patiently to get through the open bakery door. As he got closer, amazing scents wafted through the air and he understood the crowds gathering. Idly, Jack glanced through the wide, shining front window at the throng within, then stopped dead as an all-too-familiar laugh drifted to him.

Everything inside Jack went cold and still. He hadn't heard that laughter in months, but he'd have known it anywhere. Throaty, rich, it made him think of long hot nights, silk sheets and big brown eyes staring up into his in the darkness.

He'd tried to forget her. Had, he'd thought, buried the memories; yet now they came roaring back, swamping him until Jack had to fight for breath.

Even as he told himself it couldn't be her, Jack was bypassing the line and stalking into the bakery.

Don't miss
LITTLE SECRETS: HIS UNEXPECTED HEIR
by USA TODAY *bestselling author Maureen Child,*
available July 2017 wherever
Harlequin® Desire books and ebooks are sold.

www.Harlequin.com

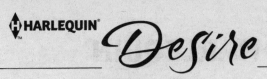

Love the Harlequin book you just read?

Your opinion matters.

Review this book on your favorite book site, review site, blog or your own social media properties and share your opinion with other readers!

Be sure to connect with us at:
Harlequin.com/Newsletters
Facebook.com/HarlequinBooks
Twitter.com/HarlequinBooks

Get 2 Free Books,
Plus 2 Free Gifts—
just for trying the
Reader Service!

HRLP17R